Taboo Sex Stories

First Time, Threesomes, Slut, Bisexual, Milfs, Anal Sex, Gangbang and Much More

Roy Loyd

Table of Contents

Let's do It Again

She was hurrying past the cabin up two doors from hers if she noticed, 'Hey there Little Red Ryder Hood...' and froze.

The deep baritone with accompanying copy allowed her past ten decades. The hair Ryder's neck climbed in a ghostly wave of handsome down blonde, and she licked off, feeling kilter already. Her eyes searched but couldn't discover the singer, till she noticed a deep gaze which slammed her into the abdomen such as a cotton-wrapped fist. 'Hubie! Joe?'

She predicted. Feeling somewhat distressed, much crazy. 'Men?' There wasn't anyway. She hadn't seen them in almost a year. No way in any way and she knew it today. Can feel it in her bones, so which hefty understanding that mimicked the sensation that she obtained after recovering from a lengthy illness like influenza or a protracted bout using a fever.

A deep understanding came. The tune which has been hummed someplace from the trees sealed the offer. It had been the boys on the market. Ryder stomped her foot.

'Hubert Sullivan Usher! Joseph Michael Palmer! Come out this second!' And she waited. Was she mad? No. They turned into the clearing, a black and tall and gruff just like a bear in a man match. Another slim and long and scenic.

Ice blue eyes and blonde hair. The boys. They'd been friends throughout college. Inseparable -- that the three of these. Friends, just, no funny business. However, for that one night.

'So no guy yet? No union, no kiddies, no picket fences? It has been almost a year old, girl,' Hubie explained. His deep voice was just like a hot hand slipping up her throat, and at the orange glow of the flame pit, Ryder shivered.

'Nope. I have a booming jewellery enterprise. I've books, friends, fantastic wine out, bills and paycheques.' She awakens. 'But none of this.' Joe smiled, his eyes somehow lurk from the luminous flash of heated mild. 'Hubie does not either, and thus don't hear him. Nor do I.' He explained the final because prissy, appropriate way that left him so endearing for her. She adored his nearly stuck-up, uptight manners. However, in Joe has been a heart of gold and a classic soul.

Along with a penis that will work wonders. Soft lips which know how to kiss. Really understand how to kiss and eat pussy. He rocked one to over one orgasm while Hubie had been. But she allowed that memory drift off to a curl of smoke. She could not move there. It was a night a long time past. Her 20th birthday. It had occurred -- only occurred -- following her salute to himself and their childhood. Her extended monologue in their love for one another and also how it would fade, since nothing lasted for.

It might fade and would their childhood. They were just likely to be younger once, just likely to appreciate each other this once. And how particular they that they'd discovered each other. Three kindred spirits, friends, nearly family but something more.

She'd let all of the muzzy-headed words slide after which she'd toasted herself and subsequently them. And the boys had shot her. No one talked about it. It had only occurred. A mixture, twist and shift of 3 bodies.

A mélange of kinds and nude components and tender words and shouts. Orgasms and skin and bliss and, in conclusion, a satiated calmness and sleep. The afternoon brought realism, and nobody had ever said it. 'selling?'

Hubie explained. Ryder shook her head and attempted to draw the words which had come until the conclusion of his sentence. She could not. 'I am sorry. I snapped out on this. What?' Hubie prevailed and cocked his head as if he was tiptoeing through her thoughts. Reliving that night long past with her.

'I stated, Ryder that the daydreamer, your jewellery, that are you promoting it' 'Oh! Tourists and a few regional news stations are buying. That is good, since then it ends up on TV and at the credits. And some regional boutiques'

'What were you thinking?' Joe said gently, smiling, poking the embers with a stick as he exploited his toe from the sand around the fire pit. His huge foot has been sheathed in his regular ship sneakers, his khaki shorts' length, his button-down shirt wrapped and pushed into his elbows.

 Regular Joe -- preppy chic. 'I had been considering the jewellery show I am doing tomorrow. How I should go off to my cottage and head to bed. I had been thinking this beer sucks butt,' she whined, carrying the last swig.

'You're thinking about people, ' Joe said, calling her bluff. 'Never,' she explained, attempting to tease her tone.

'True narrative,' Hubie grunted, agreeing with Joe. Ryder firmly refused to cave. It was one time a lifetime ago. No reason to think about doing it. At one stage they had been in you in precisely the exact same moment. You never believed that complete candy pressure could force you to come; however, it did.

You straddled Hubie and put yourself down over and again; he pulled your hands into his chest so that you might sense his heart. All the time Joe rocked to the own bottom, slipping to you about a cool river of lube. Working your butt, brushing your g-spot out of a completely new angle.

His hands-on your buttocks, holding you so that you did not float off, so it felt. Both of these. Holding you. You have never felt so secure. 'fishing,' Joe said. His grin was ornery, understanding and smart-assed. Ryder swallowed hard. After they'd been her absolute best friends. And for this one night, they'd been her fans. Something she had never been great in Hubie and Joe had been still lying. She cleared her throat and steeled her nerves to acknowledge it. 'What? I overlooked that'

Joe walked gently, drawing a heart in the sand with all the rod he held. The trick was charred out of him, poking it in the fire every couple of moments. He drank the last of the beer and explained. 'We're speaking to get a boys' weekend. Have not gotten together for weeks. Figured we would come down to a few fishing.'

'Oh,' she explained and put her empty jar on the floor. 'Yes,' Hubie stated his voice was somewhat gruff. Somewhat clogged sounding. His eyes appeared to stroke her just like a palm at the firelight -- within her breasts, her stomach, her thighs inside her lace shorts and flip-flops.

Ryder desired to eye his jeans up to find out if he'd get a hard-on however she refused. She maintained her eyes over his belt. Joe's too. 'I had better go to bed. I must get up first. Vendors will need to get there in seven sharp. Doors open at.'

She kissed them every chastely, hugged them also. She pretended to not see Joe's hard cock sucking her thigh once he dragged into the embrace. She dashed through the forests into her dark cottage and resolved to place it from her mind. For two hours she put there, not believing. Deliberately not believing. When each decadent shattered picture drifted into her head, she resolutely pushed it apart. At midnight, then she got up and poured out a glass of wine.

In 12.15 a.m, she believed it at 12.16 a.m. she banished the notion. At 12.30 a.m. she hauled in their cottage door. It had been Hubie who replied. His dark hair at a Glance along with his brow sprouted with a black blouse that meaty his tanned skin using darkness. 'Well, look what the cat dragged in,' he said gently and swung the door wide to her to go into. Ryder nevertheless wore her white nightgown. She'd pitched a grey cardigan over her feet were bare, and dirty, by the beaten path in the cottage to theirs.

'Have you been sleeping? Did you wake up? 'Hell, no, girl. We are seeing some dumb-ass film on the wire and drinking beer.'

'What film?' she asked dumbly. 'Shit if I understand.'

He touched on her lower lip, and Ryder believed her pussy go soft and liquid. A ferocious surge of bliss swelled inside her chest, and she breathed out just like he had squeezed her too tough. 'Who is there?'

She turned to watch Joe and, even if she did, her heart cried in his pale, very good looks. A grin lit his head, and she realized she loved them. After all the years. Loved that they had been, what they'd meant to her and exactly what they meant to her today.

'Small Red Ryder Hood,' Joe whispered and grabbed his arms on his chest. 'I...' Ryder dropped her words.

It had not taken long to believe that old comfortable belonging together. Something she'd seldom experienced so far in her adult life. She adored her life and her company, but she had been overlooking the rush of authentic life. The visceral response to lust and love and fucking. She did not have time.

 'You what?" Joe asked, cocking an eyebrow. 'You...?"

Hubie echoed. 'I need it ' she sighed. She blew all of the words outside on a rush of air. She had been so excited for them to listen to her that she hurried it from her mouth at a fall of speech.

'I need it back. I need back that night. That sense -- you. I need yet another night' Then she cried. Her heart was thumping like a female fighter, her throat vibration with the power of her belly dipping almost sick out of nerves. Joe turned his heels, and Hubie took her hands. What exactly did it mean?

'Come, Ry," 'Hubie stated and tugged her softly.

'We thought you would never return into the senses,' Joe said on his shoulder, and her entire body seemed to relax. It'd be okay. From the living area, it was Joe who pulled her into a hug. Engulfing her into his powerful but slender arms Hubie -- his very best friend on earth -- shut behind her.

His wide chest pressed to her back, his penis pressing on the small of her spine. Joe kissed her hands in her hair; his hard-on pushed to the cleft of her sex through the thin nightgown.

'I only need it back for an additional night,' she explained. 'We could do this,' Hubie explained, pushing his lips into her shoulder, her throat, the top layer of her mind. His cries rained down her spine, and his hands pushed her up nightie as she shivered as though she had been chilly. 'No issue,' Joe said, shoving the nightie too. Collectively they have her off the cardigan, her nightgown her panties.

She stressed temporarily, stupidly, on her filthy feet but the idea drifted off because Joe's tongue touched hers and Hubie's palms came out behind and began slow, and lazy circles on her clit.

She awakens, tasting beer Joe's tongue as his hands found her nipples and then he donned a bit too tough.

'I remember you enjoy a little annoyance,' he whined lightly and pinched her. The pain sizzled out of her breasts into her cunt and it awakens tight, tight and excited around nothing in any way. Hubie felt that the swell of her buttocks as she leaned toward Joe and said,

'Let us see if it is still correct.' He dipped his hands, each as thick around as a cigar, then deep in her pussy and then he pushed against her g-spot using an exact sort of conclusion. 'However authentic,' he said in her ear,' also flexed again.

He fell to his knees, licking a path over the curve of her spine, the bottoms of her shoulder blades, the swell of her buttocks. His palms remained buried deep into her wet pussy, his mouth never leaving her flesh. He trailed a down line till his tongue saw that the swell of her butt and he began to kiss and lick her from 1 side to another. 'not to be outdone,' said Joe, with a laugh.

He kissed down the front. His tongue was slipping in a slow, menacing dance between her breasts, over her belly. He kissed one hip bone and the other, all of them while Hubie gave attention to her buttocks. Ryder clutched at Joe, her palms buried at the light floss of the short hair. Her one hand waved wildly behind her finding buy on Hubie's shoulder. He wore nothing but cut-offs and Joe nothing but gym shorts.

They had been drinking beer watching films, she thought wildly. Minding their own business till she'd barged -- and in Joe sucked her clit in and nipped it. Difficult enough in her mind, a dark purple sizzle appeared just like a faulty blue sign. Ryder sucked air into lungs which felt too little to hold her pussy cinched tight about Hubie's thick hands.

God, how they made her feel. Singly. Together. She felt free to be than with her boys. It was that way, nevertheless appeared to be. The very first orgasm slammed it had been a blindside. One minute she felt really great, the following her cunt was fraught with waves of euphoria.

Tight, tight, tight about Hubie's probing fingers, her juices flowing out to match Joe's tongue. She held on every one of them using hands, swaying between these just like a sapling in a storm. Joe has been the first to ditch his shorts.

His penis was standing outright and accurate, ginger hair in the origin and a birthmark on his right hipbone. Hubie whined in this locker room manner along with Joe, flipped him the bird. Joe's hands cupped her buttocks, thumbing her nipples into little spikes of flesh. He brought her into the couch as Hubie fell his cut-offs. Hubie's penis was enormous. He was a huge man complete and to not be outdone at the penis department.

A delight worked through Ryder, she'd forgotten. She awakened in his thick hardon and the black hair in the bottom. His thighs, three times the magnitude of hers, looked like tree trunks.

'Do not' worry," Ryder, I will go slow,' he said, "he'd take his time. Let her correct. She nodded. She trusted Hubie along with her life, Joe too. She could surely give them an additional day of expecting them with her physique. Hubie fell like a boulder into the couch, and she sat, her back into Joe's front, and watched him stroke his penis and observe her. Subsequently, Hubie leant in and kissed her while Joe tugged her hair to create her entire scalp sing. The pain combined it together.

The kiss, the echoes of her climax. The sense of palms and mouths and cocks.

She needed them now and after and in a thousand different ways. 'I'm helpless,' she blurted. 'Great,' Hubie stated and patted his lap. She climbed. Straddling his lap because he stroked her moist slit with the head of the penis. Ryder hummed low in her throat in the feeling of flesh on flesh that is soft. Of his hard cock pressed to her exciting entry.

He held her buttocks almost reverently, and now she began to reduce herself inch at one time. Seeing as her figure swallowed his length and his mouth came hot and insistent on her toenails. Hubie little her and she jumped, however, it was Joe who whined.

'Come here, bright ass,' she stated, however, there wasn't any true heat within her name phoning. She reduced onto Hubie, her eyes drifting closed at the strain and also the fullness of being filled with him. He lifted her and lost her, then lifted her and lost her, as if she weighed nothing much greater than a bag of bread.

When he dropped, that the head of the prick nudged her g-spot, also it winked into life. Some tiny key thing waking for one more go in pleasure. Joe arrived where she pointed. Standing behind the couch that sat at the centre of the chief area, dividing the dining room space shape the TV room. He stood facing her as she awakens Hubie his penis poking impudently on the rear cushion.

Ryder took him, which means to make him endure for laughing, but if she felt that the silken slip of his hard-on within her hands, she tickles, needing nothing more than just to make him feel great -- to allow him to come. Ryder stroked Joe along with Hubie fucked her, then biting on her, so she hissed; however, her cunt went tight around his thrusting penis. She lowered her lips into Joe and kissed the tip of him that he groaned.

'A kiss?" he sighed. 'How to a French kiss?" She teased and pushed him to her mouth with her hands before sucking the length of him that he needed to shake in the rear of the couch. Hubie ceased for a minute, observing them and he then said, 'Jesus said Gonna allow me to come if I see you.'

'Do not see," Joe laughed. However, the laugh was breathy and large, as if he could not really get it out. Hubie held her buttocks tight up and whispering words which she could not quite hear. After he pushed his wide finger in her buttocks, she cried, coming.

Lips were working about Joe, who had been pushing into her mouth, losing his ways somewhat. He held double hunks of her dark red hair on his palms such as reins. 'Stop,' she said, and all of them froze. Both of these were proceeding with a larger awareness of purpose, nearly feverish.

She knew that it had been shut. It was near finish, and she said, quite calmly so that they understood she was serious, 'I would like you in me. Again. Like last moment. 'Neither of these argued. There were not any jokes jibes or teasing. This was a practically solemn but hurried rearrangement of all bodies. An almost sacred (for them, anyhow) tableau.

Hubie lay the nasty brown carpet and pulled her down. She put flush for him for a minute while Joe walked, breathing, touching his penis to remain tough. Hubie kissed his large green eyes.

'Hey, you mention the word, and it is --"Over. I understand. But I will not. I arrived at you men ' 'So you did," Little Red Ryder Hood, however.'

Ryder kissed him. Loving him protecting her, even if it intended from himself after which she sank down on him. Taking him at the next time was good, if not better, than the original. The rest had put her body on top alert. Each of the nerve endings within her pussy danced and clamoured to the sense of him.

She whispered to Joe and that he lubed himself nicely, his penis glistening with all the stuff. 'I do not need to hurt you,'" he said, pressing on the mind of himself into the tight eye of her anus.

'It always hurts at first,' he informed him, and it had been pretty much correct.

'Plus I enjoy a little bit of pain' That was pretty much accurate also. She stilled, and

Hubie held her hands on his chest. For some reason, it reminds her of praying, how he held her hands into his larger ones.

The temple of Ryder, she thought and smiled. And Joe had been in. That pinching sting of annoyance having passed simply because of breath. He began to move her shoving back, relishing the sense of getting both of these inside her body simultaneously, loving both of these.

Both of them combined physically, how they'd always appeared united emotionally and mentally. It was normal for her which was great enough to get Ryder. Along with the boys. Somehow it wasn't an embarrassing dance of three.

They discovered that rhythm of taking and give up and down and up. She strolled to orgasm just to crash down her brow into Hubie's hairy torso as he began to emerge, vibration under her if he had been delicate. Her hands in his mouth along with Joe's snaking about to press beyond her lips to the moist recesses of her mouth again.

'I missed you,' Ryder,' Hubie stated as he arrived. His enormous embarrassing buttocks tighten up so he could spoil root deep into her buttocks His heart beating so hard his rough carpet of a torso jumped beneath her palms. And Joe was together with him holding her hips and slamming. He arrived along with his lips onto her shoulder along with a straightforward,' We adore you, you understand.'

And she'd understand. That is the reason why she wanted an additional night. And that night was not over. That made Ryder grin.

The Relaxed Sex Experience

We'd been seeing each other for a few weeks. I'd pop round on the way home from school for a quick fuck, sometimes on your settee in the living room, other times on the stairs right in the hall. A couple of times you picked me up from school and took me on a short drive into the woods. Sometimes, if I had ten minutes and I was at home, I'd pop round and give you a blow job and then run back home.

After three weeks like this I managed to get away for the night. I said I was visiting a friend, left the house, went down the road, and then sneaked back up and into your house. We spent all evening in bed together. I sucked your cock and you licked my pussy for the first time. I posed for photos for you and showered with you. I took my clothes off as soon as I was through the door on Friday and didn't put them on again until I went back on Saturday evening.

One night we were lying in bed when you asked me if I'd like to go away with you for the weekend. I said yes, I'd love it, but where?

"A nudist place," you said. I thought you were joking.

"Really?"

"Yes, it's nice. Feeling the breeze against your bare skin, the grass, the bark; it's how humans are supposed to be after all."

"I suppose," I replied. "What sorts of people do you get?"

"Oh all sorts. All ages, sexes, races, and some families. What do you think?" I didn't really know, I'd never thought about it, but it was a chance to get away, and as long as they had a room we'd spend most of our time in there. I didn't imagine it would be much different to any other holiday. So I agreed.

A school friend of mine had moved away a few weeks ago and I told my parents I was going to stay with her. They drove me down to the train station, and about half an hour after they left you arrived and I got in your car. We drove for about an hour, eventually turning off the motorway onto country lanes.

"It's not far now." You said. "Actually, there's something I need to tell you." I was a little nervous "Given your age we can't say we're a couple, can we? Now, don't worry, we're still in the same room, but I've had to tell them you're my granddaughter."

I burst out laughing, "Your granddaughter?"

"Yes," you said, "pretty silly I know. Are you ok with that?"

"Sure," I said, still smiling, "that's fine."

We turned up a wooded track with the sun breaking through the leaves. We came to a gate across the narrow road with a speaker next to it on the drivers' side. You rolled your window down and pushed a button. When the answer came you said "Greenbourne and granddaughter." I laughed again as the gate opened. You looked at me and smiled too. "Behave, or I'll tell mum and dad," you said with a wink.

We parked the car, took our bags out, and walked over to a wooden building which looked like an office. There was no one around and it was very quiet, just the sounds of nature. You opened the door and I went in ahead. As my eyes adjusted from the sun to the office I was startled to see a naked man in his fifties stood in front of me.

"Hello," he said, "you must Ms. Greenbourne?" I didn't answer, I was pretty stunned as I took in what an unusual situation I'd got myself into.

"She is," you said as you came up beside me, "I'm her grandfather."

"Excellent," the naked man said, "I'm Terry, it's a pleasure to have you both here," he said, "a real pleasure." He repeated, looking at me.

Terry got the key and took us to our chalet. On the way he gave us a tour of the place. It was off season, he said, so there weren't too many people around, about

15 or so, but there was a sauna, gym, tennis courts, hot tub, and several acres of woodland we could walk in. Our chalet was small but clean, and was in a cluster of other chalets. As we went in Tony wished us a good time and said he looked forward to seeing us around the camp.

"You're very lucky to have a granddad who'll bring you somewhere like this," he said before taking one last lingering look up and down me and turning to leave.

Inside the chalet we dropped our bags and had sex straight away; me bent over the sink with you behind me and my face pushed up against the window. Afterwards, with your cum dripping out of my pussy and down my thighs, we undressed, went to the bedroom, and lay down.

"I think we'll have fun here," you said.

I smiled. "Keep doing that and we will."

You smiled too. "True Stace, but we have to go out and about round the camp as well. It will look unfriendly if we don't."

"I don't mind being unfriendly," I said "I'm here to spend time with you."

"I know Stace." You said after a pause, "Me too, but...it's something I enjoy. And you like me being happy, don't you?"

"Of course I do." I was a little upset by the idea that there was something I wouldn't do to make you happy.

"Good," you said, pausing again. "If you want me to be happy Stace, when we're out there naked, if you're sunbathing and your legs are a little spread when someone walks by, don't close them. I want us both to be totally relaxed. That's the point of this place."

A little later you decided we should take a walk. "Naked?" I asked, hoping you'd say I could take a towel or something.

"Naked." You answered. So I sat on the bed and pulled my trainers on, but was totally naked otherwise.

We stepped out of the chalet and I was all nerves in case someone saw me, I was tingling all over. It was as though my body wanted to be so sensitive it could feel even the slightest glance at me. You were relaxed and I wished I'd felt the same. As I looked round at the other chalets I froze and went cold as I saw two guys on their porches looking at me. They were sat in the shadows, out of the sun, and were at least in their 40's. I wanted to move my hands to cover my pussy and tits but, as though you could read my mind, you said softly "Remember Stace, relax."

You took my hand and led me off our porch "Afternoon." You said to the guys, and they eagerly said the same back. As we walked past their chalets to the path leading out of the clearing I could feel their eyes over every inch of my skin. Their gazes were hungry, I could almost feel them pawing at me. Part of me felt sick and embarrassed, but, to my surprise, part of me enjoyed it. My pussy tingled a little. Not only was I doing what you wanted, I also enjoyed the feeling of power I had over those guys.

We walked until we found a wide open stretch of soft grass. I brushed a space free of any twigs and lay down, and you did the same next to me. I closed my eyes, and I felt the sun and soft wind on parts of my skin I'd never felt them on before. My nipples hardened from the gentle breeze and I felt the warm rays of the sun on my vagina lips. I enjoyed the feeling and opened my legs up a little further.

I was woken up suddenly by the sound of laughing. I raised my hand to my eyes to block out the sun and saw, standing facing me, a stranger totally naked. He was about two feet from my ankles, which had spread wide apart exposing my pussy to the stranger.

"Sorry," he said to me, "didn't mean to wake you up." You were smiling as well so you two must have been talking while I slept. The stranger crouched down so he was close to me, reached out his hand and said, "I'm Glen."

"Stacey." I said shaking his hand.

"Just been talking to your granddad," he said, "shame you're only here for one night."

"Yes," I said looking at you, wondering what else you'd said.

"You have your own chalet Stace?"

"No."

"Shame," he replied before realising he might have said something wrong "You know..."

"Cheaper that way." You said.

"Yes. That's nice," Glen said, "very nice." I could see that he was staring at my bald pussy spread wide just a foot or so in front of him. I looked to you for some instructions, hoping, I think, that you would distract him or indicate I could shut my legs from his invasive gaze, but you just smiled and nodded your head slightly in Glen's direction and, instinctively, I knew what you meant. I looked at Glen's small, wrinkled cock and saw it was getting hard, its head twitching upwards.

A buzz ran right through my body seeing the effect I was having on this guy. I smiled back at you and sat up, resting with my arms behind me with my elbows on the grass, crossing my legs, and leaning far back to spread my cunt as wide as I could for him. I wondered if he could see that I was getting a little wet from showing myself off to him like this. I could see his cock take another leap upwards, which he tried to hide by facing away a little. Glen flushed, mumbled a little, and said he had to go. "If you fancy a break from you granddad come over and say hi," and he was off into the wood. When he was gone we started laughing.

"Bet he's off for a wank." You said.

"Probably," I said, "but he didn't look at my tits once."

That night was another first for me. I was washing my hands by the kitchen sink when you came over to me like you had that afternoon. You kissed my neck as I felt your stiff cock against my arse. I sighed and leaned back into you as your hands ran up from my hips, over my stomach to my tits, stroking all the way, and taking my nipples in between your thumb and finger, and rolling and squeezing them gently. My pussy was soon soaking and ready to receive you, and I offered no resistance as you bent me forwards over the sink again. I closed my eyes and smiled with anticipation as your left hand played with my left breast. I had my right hand working on my other breast and my left hand fingers rubbing my swollen clit. I couldn't wait to feel the tip of your cock against my swelled, sensitive lips.

Suddenly, I felt cold jelly on my arsehole. You were rubbing it around and poking it a centimetre or so in with the tip of your finger.

"What are you doing?" I asked.

"Shhhhh Stace." You said.

I knew what was coming, and I knew it would be painful. I took my hand from my breast and grabbed a wooden spoon by the sink. You took your hand off my tit and placed it on my shoulder, pinning it to the counter with all your weight to hold me in place. I felt the tip of your cock against my tight virgin arsehole, which had only ever had the tip of your finger up it. I thought of what your stiff seven inch cock would do to it, gulped, and closed my eyes.

"If it hurts Stace," you said "it's ok to let it out."

You were guiding your prick into my arse with your right hand gripping the base. You eased in the tip easily enough, the swollen helmet which pulsed with blood. Your finger had been about that deep in before. "Here goes," you said. I gulped again and squeezed the wooden spoon handle.

"Aaaaaaaagh!" I screamed at the unnatural, burning, tearing pain in my tight arse as your cock forced its way in. You stopped and stroked my hair.

"Shhhhh," you said, "there Stace, it'll be fine." I looked at my hand, white from squeezing the wooden spoon handle so hard, and then it was gone as my eyes closed from the pain in my arse from another deep thrust of your cock. I screamed again. Tears were streaming down my cheeks I noticed. This was worse than when you'd taken my virginity. I took some comfort from thinking that while it had hurt at the time, I was fine with it now. This would be the same, surely?

I let out another scream, which I tried to stifle by biting my lip as you pushed in again. This time you were all the way in as I could feel your pubes against my arse cheeks. I heard you grunt.

"Fucking hell," you said, "that's tight."

You didn't thrust in and out, hard and deep, as you did with my pussy, instead you rocked rhythmically backwards and forwards, our hips moving together. There was no new pain, but there was plenty left over from your entry. You stroked my hair with your left hand and held my hip with your right as you fucked my arse. I tired not to make any more noise which would put you off.

Soon the pain welled again as you pushed deep in me and I let out a deep groan. You were tensing and I knew that meant you were about to cum and you did, heavily, filling my arse with hot sticky juice.

You pulled out slowly which hurt as well. I let go of the spoon, surprised I hadn't broken it, wiped the salty tears from my cheeks and tried to stand up.

"Agh." I let out as the pain from my arse shot through me again. You pulled me close and patted my head as I buried my face in the silver hairs on your chest and sobbed.

"There there Stace, you did really well, I'm so, so proud of you." I stopped sobbing and said thanks. "That's something I really enjoy, you made me very happy." Not only was I now not sobbing, but hearing you say that actually made a smile flicker across my face. Then came a knock at the door.

"Who's that?" I asked.

"Probably some of the others here come over to say hello. It's a friendly sort of a place."

"Can you tell them to go?" I whispered weakly.

"We can't Stace," you said, "we have to be friendly back. And remember, I enjoy it here and like doing this." You looked into my eyes "It makes me happy."

"OK." I relented.

Good," you said. "They won't stay long. Go off to the bathroom and clean yourself up a little. Remember, you're my granddaughter." I walked painfully to the bathroom.

I shut the door behind me, wiped my face and straightened my hair a little. I could feel your cum seeping out of my arse, so I pulled some toilet roll and ran it gently up in my arse crack. I looked down at the paper to see cum mixed in with blood. I dropped it in the toilet, ran another handful and did it again. I repeated this a couple more times then flushed. I looked at myself in the mirror once more. I looked ok, but the pain in my arse was throbbing and burning. I took a deep breath and went back out into the living room, trying to hide the pain as best as I could.

Sitting around with you were Glen, Terry, and another couple of guys. "Stace," you said, "you know Glen and Terry, this is John and Mark, they're in the chalet two down."

They both said hi and I managed to reply. The two of them, and Glen and Terry, were staring at me like they had been this morning. I immediately became very self conscious about being stood totally naked in front of them.

"Take a seat Stace." You said. I couldn't really say no, and the only seat was on the small sofa in between John and Mark. I walked over, hiding the pain in my arse, their eyes roaming over me all the way. I came in between them, turned my back and taking a deep breath began to lower myself onto the sofa. The pain was incredible but I managed it.

The gap between John and Mark was so small that my hips were pressed against theirs. Both continued to stare at me, and neither made any attempt to hide the fact that they had solid erections. Neither did Glen or Terry for that matter. I was turned on as before to discover the power my body and sexuality had over these men and my nipples hardened but the pain I was in stopped my enjoying it as much as I would have otherwise.

"Your granddad was telling us you have to keep this secret from your parents," said Glen. I nodded.

"Yes," I said. It was kind of true.

"Do you have any other secrets?" Mark asked. As I turned to face him he made a big point of looking me up and down.

"Then they wouldn't be secrets," you told him.

"There was quite a bit of noise coming from in here just now," Terry said, "everything ok?"

"Yes," you replied. "We were taking a splinter from her foot." I noticed that John had snuck his arm around behind my shoulders.

"Is it just me or is it hot in here?" he asked with a wink. The others giggled like schoolboys.

"It is a bit warm," you said. "Stace, maybe you could get us some drinks from the fridge?" I didn't much like the thought of getting up and walking around given the pain I was in, but it got me away from Mark and John so I took another deep breath and pulled myself up, the two guys making a close inspection of my arse as I did so. I kept my cheeks tightly clenched and headed for the fridge.

"You're a lucky man to have a maid like that." Mark said to you and I heard you all laugh behind my back. I shut the fridge door and came back with five bottles of water. I stood in front of you all and crouched to put the bottles on the floor. The pain shot through me again, though a little less than before. I was beginning to recover. I took the top off one and handed it to you. Then I turned and handed one each to Mark and John. Then I heard Terry behind me cough rather obviously. I turned to him and he was looking at you so I switched my gaze to you wondering what was going on.

"Er...Stace" you said indicating the floor underneath where I was crouching. I looked down, and a wave of shame and embarrassment hit me so physically that I could feel my skin burning as I saw a few drops of blood. I stood up and headed straight for the bedroom and as I shut the door I heard sniggering behind me. I curled up on our bed and cried. Not for the pain or embarrassment, but because I felt I had let you down.

That night my arse was still sore, so you lay me face down on the bed and spread my legs. You put some more of the jelly on your little finger and worked it into my anus. It hurt, but as you pulled it out and pushed it in slowly the cool jelly made the burning go away a little. You stroked my hair softly with your other hand. Soon I began to drift off to sleep, with the breeze fluttering through the curtain by the open window, and your finger still gently working me, stretching my sphincter. We were going home tomorrow. "I hope I'll be better for the netball match on Tuesday," was the last thought I remember before falling asleep.

Tempting Defiance

On February fourteenth, Alicia and Anthony had organized an erotic and passionate rendezvous at his manor, his playground. When they discussed and planned their arrangements for the ecstatic carnal adventures, Anthony had specifically instructed Alicia not to invigorate herself at all amidst the day prior to their meeting... His hard-coded rule denied Alicia the luxury of nipple play, pussy play, and clitoral play. He wanted her to be intensely stimulated and savagely consumed by her own wild sexual urges when he would show up. Although she reluctantly consented, the subtle vibrations in her voice advised his intuition that she wouldn't comply. Anthony realized that Alicia would shower for him just before his planned visit. She always loved how much Anthony appreciated the fragrance of her freshly showered body, untainted by salve, perfume or cologne... It inflamed the raw passion that invigorated him to take her from that fresh bathed fragrance to the enticing and intoxicating aroma of sweat and pleasure juices that ultimately seeped as their amorous adventures progressed. Frequently he could smell her ecstatic fervor even before he saw its physical signs.

Arriving much earlier than the scheduled time, Anthony patiently waited outside his villa until he saw the washroom light in Alicia's room turned on. Standing in the patio garden, he keenly noticed her developments, behind the frosted glass of the window. Slowly and steadily, Alicia walked into the shower. It was his manor; he always had a set of extra keys. Without wasting any further time, he rushed to the back door of the manor and let himself in.

He secretly tiptoed through the living room and into the bedroom. As of now, Alicia had lit the candles dissipated all through the room. The atmosphere within the room was dark as it patiently, yet impatiently waited for the initiation of the dark fantasy games to enlighten itself. Indeed, even the light from the washroom was excessively insufficient to illuminate the corridor or any other part of the room. "Perfect", Anthony thought inwardly as he breathed in the scent of the room-freshener and the scented candles all around intoxicating him further. The restroom door was all the way open and Anthony stood simply at the entrance of the corridor, watching Alicia as she showered. For a moment, the seductive curves and tempting edges of charming temptress doped his mind. She moved earnestly under the shower as she typically did; wetting all her body aside from her long, thick and dense hair. Jetted and thick streams of water washed her lush framework, from the neck, then her shoulders, then streamed down her succulent udders, her navel and ultimately down to the joint between her legs. Anthony let her eyes devour the raw seduction of his attractive slave, as her long and sexy fingers lingered on her nipples. His manhood throbbed a little as he witnessed the temptation of his slave growing, a spectacular and thrilling sight not to happen too easily. For a moment, Alicia was nearly enticed to play with her nipples. Her edginess sent raw impulses through her veins inciting her, provoking her to deny the guidelines of the game. "An audacious behavior worthy to be punished Alicia severely, watch it!" Her devious mind screamed in her ears, "Girl, you love to be punished, don't you? You love his attention all the time, don't you." But, the angel overpowered the devil this time as another part of his mind spoke, "You are true to your master, aren't you Alicia?" She shook her head as if trying to liberate her mind from that extremely enticing thought of self-play and continued with her bathing.

Alicia always knew the amount Anthony adored her smooth legs. As she recalled past sensual adventures and crafted the forthcoming one in her psyche, she lathered her legs with shaving cream and kept on shaving each one smoothly with the most extreme consideration. She needed to prepare herself before her master showed up. Slowly and steadily, she shaved the joint in between her legs and invested a ton of energy, guaranteed that it was perfectly clean like of a teenager. Smooth legs, neatly shaven pussy; she laughed as she completed her beautification pleased to show her lavish framework to her master to be ravished and used for his pleasure. And, that pride caused her downfall. Finally, the devil had overpowered the Angel. Snatching the after to shaving cream, she cautiously applied the strawberry flavored liquid all over her skin. As Alicia massaged it within her left thigh, Anthony keenly noticed that her hand paused and waited over her pubis. He saw her reclining against the washroom wall. Having such large numbers of carnal adventures before this planned one, Anthony knew her groans like the lines of his palm. In this manner, when Alicia groaned in that husky tone, Anthony detected the groan he had heard so frequently before and during fulfilling their savage wants. That groan only implied that his slave had defined his orders, extended the labia back over her clit with two fingers of one hand, while the middle finger of her other hand delicately brushed the core peeking out from that solidly extended tissue.

With that, Anthony walked silently to the shower and stood directly before the entryway. Alicia's eyes were closed in fervor envisioning sensual illustrations of raw passion. The door creaked as Anthony twisted the knob to open the door completely and Alicia's erotic imaginations were overwhelmed at that very clamor. She gasped in terror perceiving that her master Anthony had caught her red-handed in the act of sheer defiance of his orders and wishes. Without uttering a single word, Anthony held his hand out for her to take. Alicia was trembling with anxiety still uncertain of her master's state of mind. "Shit Alicia! You wretched fool! Is he angry with me? What's he going to do to me? Fuck it, Ali! How could you be so careless?" Alicia cursed herself as her mind continued racing from one idea to another. All at once, the environment in the shower felt so damn cold or was she freezing in sheer dread. Her mind and body were bewildered with an uneasy blend of fear and wild excitement. With trembling hands, Alicia reached her hand out to him and left the shower. Still quiet and without articulating a word, Anthony grabbed the large shower towel off the towel bar and began to get her dry. Although he wasn't harsh, he was cautious and careful in his approach. She gasped as the coarseness of the towel scratched over her erect nipples. Alicia was obedient like a child as Anthony ordered that she bend over and used her hands to spread her butt cheeks so that he could make her that place dry too. In that process, he caused her squat somewhat so that he could also clean in between her legs as well. As the rough texture of the towel scoured quickly over her previously stimulated pussy, she was gasping with hardly a pause in between.

"Come, my little dove," Anthony commanded as he turned and tossed the towel onto the floor.

"B…B…But," Alicia stammered.

His furious and cold look squashed the protest on her lips, and she knew her endeavors of pleading would yield her no results.

As they walked back into the room, he pulled the heavy weighted oak seat from its place at the workspace. She realized what it implied, to spread her legs wide and bend over on the seat. For a moment, Alicia had her musings racing from one thought to another pondering the most exceedingly awful possible outcomes. "An over-the-knee spanking? Electrical stimulation on the pussy? An ice cube treatment in both her pits? Definitely, he isn't that irritated with me," Alicia attempted to compose herself as she inhaled deeply.

As he opened the closet containing their different toys, she stood awfully frightened. As he examined those different instruments, she eagerly looked at him with dread-filled eyes. Anthony watched his little dove with unmistakable fascination and amusement from the corner of his eyes. He held each gear in the stock just to tease her fantasies, investigated them with keen interest just to elevate her tension. Some he returned into the closet, others he laid on the dresser.

Finally, Anthony grabbed the blindfold. Alicia looked with fear in her eyes. The Blindfold. It constantly inflamed a degree of extreme enthusiasm in her. She generally feared it, yet she couldn't deny it each time it was put to play. He kept her standing behind the seat, gripping the chair-back and then, he slipped the blindfold into the spot. He stood quietly, watching her reaction. She inhaled hard as the darkness descended blocking her sight yet escalating her wild fantasies. Her pulse, recognizable at the base of her neck, increased surprisingly. Her nipples hardened fully expecting a fascinating lustful storm.

Alicia stood grasping the seat and listened cautiously as Anthony moved back to the dresser. Her heartbeat pounded like bass drums when she heard his strides returning to her. Yes, he returned and took her hands in his.

"Bend over," Anthony commanded her as he pulled her hands down toward the seat. Alicia felt the peak of the seat back, squeezing into her stomach as she bent over. Her nipples were more invigorated and erect as the heaviness of her superbly formed udders followed gravity as she bent. She gripped the edges of the seat.

"S-s-s-s-s-o-a-a-h!" Alicia wheezed as she felt the rope circumvent her wrists and pulled tight. She was restrained to the seat hand rest. Anthony left again and she had her ears on high alert once more. Detecting a cling of some metal on wood, she understood his essence behind her.

His hand gripped her ankle. "Spread them," He growled, pinching within her thigh until she had her legs spread wide apart. Again Alicia whimpered as Anthony restrained her ankles to the legs of the chair. Anthony had his little dove absolutely restrained; her hands were bound, her legs were widely separated, uncovering her sex pits completely. Alicia heaved as her senses were vanquished by raw wants. "What's he going to do straightaway? Spank me? Give me a finger fuck? Gag me on his cock?" Restrained, blindfolded, she didn't know whether the first touch of her master would be the arousing touch of his hands, the stirring touch of Valentine's Day rose, or a hard smack of his belt. She just knew the idea of any of her fantasies would make her unbelievably aroused. The more she contemplated, the greater was her submission moistening her. Anthony smelled his little dove's arousal. The musk of her pussy, the sweet drops perspiring under her arms and her brow; indeed, he could smell her. He understood she yearned for this, craved for this, and needed this desperately. He strolled a foot back and give her a chance to gather her senses. Alicia was his. Alicia had no control. There she was dripping with savage wants and desires and yearning for his touch to calm her fire.

"I'm going to give you what you were hungry for and what I need," Anthony murmured in her ears. Goosebumps coursed through her lavish skin enraging her desires.

To show this, Anthony ran his hands over her body. He took ample and serious time while he caressed her hardened nipples, kneaded them, squeezed them, and stimulated them until Alicia kicked her hips to express her desperate needs. He ran his hands between her legs and slipped his finger into the hot dripping pit of her burning pussy. Alicia was dribbling her wants as they traced their way through her inner thighs. His fingers felt like magic when he explored her wetness; nearly dragging her to the zeniths of excitements. "Come little dove, here, taste yourself," he teased as he took his fingers in the vicinity of her mouth. Alicia snaked her tongue out, she found his fingers beyond her reach, she was going insane. Anthony continued his teases and just placed the finger on her luscious lips, she devoured her salty juices. She was going insane.

Anthony nestled her ear, "I now own your body slut, your mind, your soul," he murmured. "You're mine to do whatever I see fit. I'm your master, your God, your worst and terrible nightmare... The Devil and the architect of your devious wants."

Besides, to exhibit to her that she was just his, Anthony took his left thumb and index finger and spread the fleshy cheeks of her butts.

"O-goodness, p-please n-no" Alicia stammered, recognizing what would occur.

Of course, his fingers attacked the profundities of her womanhood getting greased up in her dampness. Waves after waves of exquisite erotica smashed on the edges of her curves as she trembled with lust. Her thighs trembled as her rosebuds enveloped every inch of his strong fingers. Her body burned with intense lust as she shook violently. At that point, he pulled his finger from her pussy and slowly scoured the juices over her butt. She was not used to this so early. This act generally came somewhat later, when she needed it. Not at the earliest time. She was not ready.

"A-h-o-h-h-h-h! G-g-g-o-d, Ah! O-goodness o-i-i-h, p-please!" Alicia screamed as his well-greased up middle finger penetrated her ass to the knuckle.

"What did I tell you?" Anthony asked calmly.

"A-h-h! P-please! I won't d-do Y a-n a-h!" She inhaled hard as if the air was being blocked from her lungs. She was getting choked without the gags or muffles. Anthony pulled his middle finger out of her anal pit, but only to thrust it back again.

"What did I tell you?" He asked once more, this time sterner, somewhat agitated; Alicia froze as his voice resonated in her ears.

"Wh-h-h-o-o-o-o!" she groaned understanding the warmth growing strongly in her pussy, "N-not Not to d-do an-any-t-thing w-with m-my p-pussy!"

"Yes...Without a doubt," Anthony concurred, "And now you should pay the cost of defiance."

"Please, Sir! If you p-please! I just W-whaaa!" she shrieked as he stroked his finger in and out again.

"I hate excuses, little dove". He snarled, "Would you say you are ready to start and pay the price?"

She crashed onto the harsh grounds of reality. "Ready to start and pay the price?" She pondered alarmed and terrified as goosebumps coursed all over her skin. "We haven't started yet?"

She groaned in an exquisite blend of relief and frustration as his finger slid out of her ass. She protested when it was inside her, yet the reality of the situation was, she ached for it, she was desperate for her master's touch, she longed to satisfy his craving.

She felt him standing before her and his hand lifted her chin up. She felt the shine, the grasping warmth and passionate comfort of his breath as his lips spread hers.

The kiss she pondered in sheer anxiousness.

The kiss always denoted the initiation of their play.

His lips waited on hers and she opened hers marginally to let his tongue slid into her mouth. His hands moved from supporting her face to brushing the tips of her hardened nipples as they hung tight the ends of her succulent udders. He snatched the back of her head with one hand and pulled her back more earnestly to him, finally taking her breath away and blowing her mind. She forgot whose air, she took in as her senses ached for more lust, want and need as he kept on folding his lips and tongue around her luscious and enticing ones.

"You understand how much I love you," He expressed politely, yet sternly, and she sensed that his voice was filled with expectation.

"Yes, indeed," Alicia mumbled; while her heart pounding like drums.

Right then and there, she felt the blistering torment as the first nipple clip teethed its ideal place.

"S-s-s-s-s-o-o-o-h-h-a-r-r-r-g-g-h-h!" Alicia inhaled hard and fast as the teeth of the first nipple clip bit into the erect pap of her left nipple.

"Oh-h-h-i-i-o-n-n-n-g-g-g-g an ah!" she groaned as she felt the next nipple clip nibble into the fragile erect nub of her right nipple.

Driving herself to breathe in profoundly through her nose, she permitted the air an opportunity to fill her lungs. She waited enthusiastically for the underlying excruciating agony to pass by, but to her sheer surprise, she was getting excited by the consistent throb she so frantically required. Slowly the agonizing pain settled in and she groaned in ecstatic delight as the sensation moved from her delicate nipples down her spine, wandering to her pussy, settling there and making her wiggle her hips in desperation.

In any case, Anthony wasn't done with the nipple play. For some time, Alicia thought she felt something other than the vibe of the clamps. There seemed to be some sort of drag along with the gravity on them. Actually, each clamp had been attached to a little chain fit for holding minor, yet exceptionally overpowering weights. He carefully attached weights at the end of each chain. She realized that something would happen, she yet wasn't prepared for the stun of anguish that coursed through her body when he held the loads up and after that dropped them along with gravity with the expectation that they snapped her delicate nipples straight down.

"Y-e-e-e-e-o-o-o-w-w! O-o-o-h-h-h, a-a-a-r-r-r-g-g-h-g-g-god! Oh my god, p-please!" she shouted as the weights swung back and forth pulling the nipple clamps, the teeth solidly gritted on every now red pap which was pulled and stretched out toward the end of her tits. Again, there was this disrupting pause; again the impatient wait that would allow her to settle in the blistering torment. Her pussy was throbbing in desperate cravings and started to ooze her excitements. Alicia felt it streaming down within her widely extended thighs and felt humiliated at the possibility of her uncontrolled stimulations and electrified stirrings.

As she moved her body, marginally to adjust her agony and control her excitement, she was immediately welcomed with another shock of intense pain when the weights on the nipple clamps swung to the ends of her nipple. "Ahh-h-o-o-o-h-u-u-n-n-h!" She groaned.

Anthony stood aside, discreetly watching her as she raved up in her torment. He smiled in intense joy and supreme delight as he saw her thighs smoothening with her juices. Alicia was starting to spill and she had so far to go he thought inwardly as he moved back to the closet.

He reached in and grabbed a little container of lotion alongside a medium-sized butt plug. Alicia always adored and admired anal, cherished each ounce of it, but she was little in her anal cavity and he was always careful not to use the enormous fittings. There is clearly a fine line between pain and injury and he was responsible enough to stay away from the later without any doubts.

Anthony turned and walked around to her. "You defied an order, did you not?" he inquired.

"Indeed, I did," she answered nodding her head enthusiastically in affirmation.

"You understand you must be punished..." Anthony expressed harshly.

"Yes," she nodded again as her heart began to pound at the ominous reverberation in his voice.

"Be that as it may, I have got an arrangement for you dove. I need you at my mercy. I want to make you purr." Anthony murmured in her ears. Goosebumps followed its course through the gleaming sweating skin of Alicia as she trembled at her master's wishes. Her heart was desperate to feel what she craved the most. She couldn't rationalize it; it was simply wild desire, raw passionate lust. She had faith in lust and love. Her mind was out of her control to summarize love, desire, sex, and feelings to a fair equation. She lusted for the mess and chaos. She lusted for Anthony to go insane for her. She wanted to feel the enthusiasm, the warmth, the sweat, and the madness. Actually, she required them all.

Saying nothing further, Anthony moved behind her. She attempted to move in nervousness and then panted when he slowly and gradually leaked the lotion into the split of her ass cheeks allowing it to run down and run over the wrinkled rose of her butt.

"A-a-a-h-h-h, p-please" Alicia mumbled, "Ah-please d-don't".

"Too late, little dove," he replied, "You defied an order. Your audacity must be punished."

"O-h-h-h," she inhaled hard and fast as he utilized his middle finger to spread the lotion over her butt, "E-e-e-c-h!" Alicia shouted in a mind-boggling mix of delight and pain as he pushed his finger inside her, again penetrating her to the knuckle. At that point, he immediately pulled his finger and grabbed the butt-plug.

It was around 4 inches long; it began as a blunt point that step by step expanded in size until it was around 1 inch in diameter. At that point, it diminished quickly to a tight neck that closed in a wide base. The design was impeccable with the ultimate objective that it all together expanded the anal cavity of the wearer as it penetrated. Then, it enabled it to close around the fitting and held it in place, while the wide base kept it from totally vanishing into the anal fissure. The result was a fundamental stretching joined by significant distress followed by a loosening up of the rear-end and a much satisfied ecstatic inclination.

"A-h-h-h-h-h!" Alicia wheezed as he utilized his thumb and index finger to spread her butt cheeks and totally reveal the winking cavity of her rear-end.

"U-n-n-n-n-h-h!" Alicia snorted as she detected him to place the tip of the butt plug at which she felt, by all means, the core of her body.

Anthony worked the butt plug about an inch inside and after that gave her a chance to push it back out. She screeched as she felt the fitting beginning the underlying stretching, kicking her hips accordingly, then screeching again as the internal penetration set the weights attached to her nipple clamps swinging.

Again, he pushed the butt plug into the anal cavity further. "A-r-r-r-g-g-g-h-h, o g-god, p-p-pleeeease! N-no, p-pleeease!" Alicia screeched as she felt it stretching her butt until she saw red before her blindfolded eyes.

Again he allowed her to push it back out. She was wheezing and kicking against her restraints, yet striving hard to keep still, desperate to decrease the movement of the weights dangling from her nipples.

"Y-e-e-e-e-c-c-c-h-h-h! A-h-h-h-h, u-n-n-n-h-h-g-g, oh god! n-n-n-oooo! Wh a-n a-!" Alicia hollered as she shivered wildly in agony as the most extensive part of the butt plug was pressed into her. At that point, she gasped in relief as the shoulder of the butt plug infiltrated her rear-end and she felt her ass gripping around the thin neck. The base of the butt plug settled comfortably into her anal pit. She was covered in a fine sheen of sweat and breathing erratically faster in an ideal blend of pain and pleasure. Her pussy was literally spilling now and she felt the juices running down her calves. Her rear end was full, her tits were stretched out far and burning with a blistering sensation, but, she frantically desired to cum, her hips bucking in a regular fucking rhythm, be that as it may, her legs were stretched so far apart that she could feel no friction on her clit. Alicia cried in distressful frustration and an intensified arousal.

Anthony allowed her no rest. Without squandering any further minute, he grabbed a wide leather paddle resembling the design of a tennis racket. Anthony held it directly before her nose so that she could breathe in the scent of leather; she could take in the fragrance of her perspiration on the leather paddle of their past carnal encounters.

"Goodness! No! N-n-oo-t now!" Alicia pleaded desperately, "Not the paddle! Please, I'm so sorry, not the paddle. I have a butt plug in my ass, please not the paddle with a butt plug".

"You can beg better, little dove," he countered, "Possibly you'll consider this whenever you dare to disobey and defy again in future."

With that, he strolled behind her and taking his measure, brought the paddle over her upturned ass with a sharp S-P-A-N-K!

"W-hh-y-y-y-y-e-e-e-e-e!" Alicia shouted as the blistering warmth from the paddle burned her ass cheeks with a severely bitter sensation. Her butt plug plunged somewhat deeper into her anal pit at the thud of the paddle and she wheezed at the exciting fulfilling sensation it resonated. The weights swung strongly and clicked together, snapping the ever-sensitive stubs on her chests. Her pussy sobbed and she kicked her hips hopelessly wanting for her ecstatic sexual discharge. Regardless of her arousals, she was a long way from the pinnacles of her climaxes.

S-P-A-N-K the paddle crashed another blistering thud again...

Anthony was not in a mood to let her relax.

He stayed by her, giving her a chance to adjust the torment. Alicia was squirming her ass in a painfully disturbed and traumatic agitating state. Two expansive stripes of red lay glimmering over the broadest region of her upturned hips. She was again in extreme desperation to calm her excitements by breathing in profoundly and rapidly through her nose. Her nipples burned with a blistering sensation blending with agony and delight, the nipple clips and weights kept on making their essence felt as the weighted teeth pulled relentlessly at her delicate and stretched out nipples.

Her ass was gripping around the base of the butt plug, with each constriction came a surge of exciting sexual agitation. All she could pray to God was for to help her cross the limits of her sexual zeniths; however, Anthony was too mindful about his pet play to even consider turning off the heat so soon.

Anthony stepped forward, measured her ass cheeks with the leather paddle once again and utilizing an uppercut stroke, delivered another extremely powerful thud of the leather paddle onto the underside of her butt cheeks.

"Y a-n a-h-h-h!" Alicia yelled ascending on her toes; her lower calf muscles flexing hard in wretched strains to lift her ass a long way from the rapidly made horrendous warmth conquering her butts.

S-p-a-n-k! Another severe vicious stroke crossed the underside of her ass.

"Y-l-l-l-e-e-e-e!" Alicia shrilled tossing her head back and lifting her up on her toes again as if she was lifting herself to the pinnacle of her sexual pleasures. "Goodness, p-p-pl-e-e-e-ase!" she faltered. Furthermore, with that, she understood her orgasm building. "One more, please if you can hit once more", her mind screamed in frustration and desperation to throw her off the edges of sexual peaks, "Just one more", she desperately pleaded in her mind.

Anthony sensed it too. Now is the right time.

He delivered the last incredible severe thud with another horrible undercut...

"O-G-O-D, Y-yes-s-s-s-s!" she wheezed as she raised herself up on her toes once and for all and her body went rigid. Her orgasm washed over her in what was apparently a perpetual wave. The agony, the warmth, the thrilling sensual ecstasies all blended perfectly into an orgy of conflicting, yet complementary feelings. She shuddered wildly shaking the heavy weighted oak chair as waves after waves of electrifying delights flooded through the pits of her lush seduction.

Anthony stood back and saw her orgasm progressing from the first unique savage compressions to shudders of a quiet gasping. As Alicia settled, Anthony hurried to release his little bird from the nipple cinches and hanging loads. Alicia felt his fingers in her butt and she pushed to assist him with expelling her butt plug. Obviously, it came out easily. He untied her bonds and lifted her in his solid arms, carried her, still blindfolded, to the bed. Alicia sat and after that fell on her back. Anthony undressed rapidly and he settled beside her. He lifted the blindfold and she looked at him. "Thank you, Sir!" she mumbled. He turned her so her back was supported against his sturdy stomach and his throbbing manhood penetrated the pit of her womanhood. Their gasps of another raw, passionate ecstasy were simultaneous. Her hands clawed for a handhold on the sheets as he took her. He yanked his hand in her hair and pulled her back, her mouth open in a soundless scream. An airless breath. She had no imaginations, no idea, and no thoughts. She could just feel.

A MILFs Revenge Sex Story

Life changes and we must either change with it or get left behind. That's what my grandparents used to tell me when I was a teenager. It's funny how you can be reminded of such things at just the perfect time when life throws a curve towards you. Recently I found myself confronted with one of these situations where I had to admit that life had drastically changed in one of the most heartbreaking ways possible and then decide how to react. The way I chose to respond is easily the craziest thing I have ever done but also something I am very happy about. It's not for the faint of heart.

My name is Ericka and I am a forty-one year old mother of two. I've been married to the same wonderful man for fifteen years and life couldn't have played out better if I was allowed to order it through a catalog. Though I do keep busy with my job as the lead administrative assistant for a local engineering firm, I enjoy time with my family most of all.

Hank has been a loving, supportive and loyal husband for the entirety of our marriage. We have squabbles of course but who doesn't right? I couldn't have asked for a better partner through the last decade and half. My kids are doing well in school. Jeanie is in the honors society in high school and Marcus seems to be hell bent on blazing a path all his own as he plans to become a professional artist one day.

Life together has trained Hank and I to become a fifty – fifty team in all things around the house, including cooking. I make breakfast and get the lunches ready for the day while he gets home before I do and fixes whatever we choose for dinner every night and helps with any homework issues that might arise. I like to take a spin in the gym every afternoon to make sure I keep myself in top physical condition. Or as top condition as there is at my age with two kids, and Hank always doing his part around the house in the afternoons has always allowed me the ability to do that. It isn't like he doesn't get benefits though because the healthier I feel every day, the happier and more satisfying Hank's nights are as well. Let's just say that we are happy to have our master sweet on the complete other side of the house from the kids.

That's what normal is for me. Well, I'll back up on that a little bit. That is what life was like for me up until a couple of months ago. Things changed around that time for Hank and me.

It was a Thursday and Hank and I had been going through one of those tough spells that married couples go through now and then. He was being stupid about something and I was in turn being equally block-headed about forgiving him and forgetting it. Really it was a lot like most of our little squabbles over the years until that day when things changed. He didn't call me that afternoon to work out what we were going to do for dinner.

Hank never could decide what kind of food he was in the mood for, so I left it up to him most of the time and he never missed a call until that day. Odd as it was, I made sure to call him a couple of times and then texted several times when there was no answer. When no reply came from the texts, I called his office and asked to talk to him. Becky, one of his supervisors, said that he had taken off at lunch so that he could take care of some personal business during the afternoon.

Personal business? I wanted to demand of her what kind of personal business he was into that his wife wouldn't know about, but I didn't for fear it would get Hank in some kind of trouble. Then I began to worry if he had found some kind of trouble on his own that afternoon. It wasn't like him to miss a call.

I began to hope he had simply gone to purchase tickets to the movie I had been talking about wanting to see or maybe even a couple of weekend passes to the big monster truck rally happening at the coliseum for himself and our youngest son. I was of course completely kidding myself but what other choice did I have? Things that the little nagging voice in the back of my mind was telling me just didn't make sense. Sure affairs were tragic and terrible but they happen to people who I know and even a close friend or two. They damn sure don't happen to me. Hank wouldn't do that to me; he couldn't.

But then I sort of laughed at the way my mind was playing tricks on me. It was only one Thursday afternoon and he would probably have a good explanation for what had happened. So I waited for him to come home. I waited and waited all night until he finally stumbled in the door a few minutes after eleven. He was clearly drunk and smelled like he had spent all night in a bar with a bunch of crazies. I stood there as his gaze finally caught mine and simply said, "Goodnight, Hank," before turning and going to bed.

That was the start and boy was it ever a bad start. The next few days were a little too good with Hank as he was trying too hard to fix whatever bit of stupid he had done that night but it didn't last. Shortly things were back to normal for about thirty-six hours before he suddenly went missing again one night. I waited up until midnight that night watching recorded detective shows on the DVR. He walked in looking and smelling much the same as the first night and I almost confronted him about what the hell he had gotten into but I decided against it at the last moment.

It was possible that something strange was going on, or so the overly optimistic side of me kept saying. Over the first month his rebound days were fewer and his nights going missing doubled and then tripled.

Finally after almost two solid months of the mess I decided enough was enough. My best friend Jill suggested that I follow him around to confirm where he was going but I said to hell with that. While I appreciated her trying to help, I wasn't about to waste time and energy chasing my husband around town to confirm what was obvious. The bastard was going to have to come clean all by himself like a big boy. At the last minute I did decide to add a little flavor to my confrontation by wearing one of my skimpiest lingerie and a loose silk robe.

Glancing in the mirror confirmed how good I looked. I still keep my blonde hair long and on humid days the natural wave nearly becomes a curl that cascades a few inches past my shoulders. My blue eyes held something of a mysterious glare when I wanted them to and my body was well respectable and not just for my age. I had great genes which had always allowed me to stay thin and the workouts I regularly did kept me in good shape on top of that. Without being too arrogant about it, I could see why I garnered a lot of attention when my work took me across college campuses.

That look, complete with the awesome red lingerie was what awaited Hank when he walked into the room and it sobered him up with a start. A similar situation in the past might have seen him turn and lock the bedroom door for good measure before quickly stripping his clothes off and joining me in bed. This time was different of course.

"Oh, shit," he panted a time or two, "You look great babe but I am so..."

"Drunk?" I interrupted, "Tired? Spent? Fucked? Have you shot your load already dear? I know you usually only have the one."

He shook his head and propped his hand on the door facing, "Fuck. So you know."

"No, darling," I said in sarcasm, "I don't know. Whatever are you talking about?

You mean the way you suddenly started going missing a few nights each week a couple of months ago? The way you smell like a shitty bar and a cheap whore when you come home late on those nights? Or is it the way you have stopped touching me or even looking at me with desire for the first time in our marriage? Which part do I know Hank?"

Suddenly his face changed as if he had decided to go on the offensive and he threw his hands up, "Okay, you want to do this right now? Fine. I have met someone, a girl barely over thirty and I have been spending time with her. She is wild and crazy and has shown me things that you never could."

It hurt like a knife being driven through me but I only allowed a few quiet tears to ease out before I hit back. "How would you know how wild I can be Hank? You seemed pretty damn satisfied up until you met this hussy! I don't care if she is an eighteen year old supermodel, you can't do much better than me Hank and you knew that once."

"I Wanted something more!" he yelled.

"You never said a damn word about that to me, your wife, you idiot! How do you know what I would be willing or unwilling to do for you? You have no idea what kind of fantasies I have had and yet stayed loyal to you. Twice a week I find myself in meetings on college campuses around the state. You talk about barely over thirty, sweetheart, I get looks of drooling desire from college hunks all the damn time and have for years! Yet, never have I even entertained the idea of being unfaithful to you and this is how you repay me?"

He didn't immediately answer and I knew why, "Oh, it bothers you that younger men find me attractive. You want to claim me as some property? We are married you stupid idiot. You don't have to claim me to have me. I am right here and have been for fifteen fucking years! How hard have you worked and how much crazy crap have you done just to try to be more pleasurable to this young slut? Did you ever imagine, ever think for one second what you might get from me if you tried that hard right here in your own bedroom?"

"Oh, come on," he said flippantly, "You are so conservative that you couldn't let yourself do crazy stuff like the younger girls do, like this girl does for me."

"It's not hard to pour booze down your throat and dump ash trays all over you so you smell like smoking shit, dear. I could do that."

Hank waved a hand at me, "You know what I mean, in the bed, having sex. I've had sex in public Ericka. You know you would never do that."

I looked down and wiped the hurt away from my face for a moment as I walked towards his underwear drawer and grabbed something clean. Walking over to the linen closet, I grabbed a towel and washcloth and handed it all to him with a stern expression on my face. "You'll need to shower in the guest bath before sleeping on the couch Hank. You never said you wanted to do wild sexual things in public, Hank. You never even considered asking me what I was willing or able to do for you, my husband. But that's okay. You want to know what I can do? Want to know what I am capable of doing? Enjoy your younger hussy and get a front row seat if you want. I'll show you what this body can do you cheating bastard." With that I pushed him threw the doorway then shut and locked the door.

That is more or less how it went and I drew strength from the look of surprise and worry on his face when I shut the door as I lay in bed crying myself to sleep. I could tell you that I was only pissed off but that would be a lie. This is my husband we are talking about who did something to me that I never even considered was a possibility for us so yeah, I was heartbroken. It hurt badly what he had done to me. Such insulting betrayal to find sex somewhere else and claim that I was unwilling or even unable to please him like whatever slut he had found. It wasn't only heartbreak that I felt though. You better believe that I was mad as hell and already thinking how sweat it would be to get revenge on his ass.

The following Thursday was a day I was going to be on campus at a local college and I told Hank and the kids that I would be grinding hard on the college campuses that day and that they would have to figure out dinner. A wink towards Hank let him know exactly what I meant and I enjoyed the irritated look on his face as I left for work.

The engineering firm I work for does a ton of work on colleges around the state, so much in fact that they don't have enough important engineering types to attend all of the meetings. A couple of years ago my boss asked me if I would be willing to accept a small promotion that would mean my going to planning meetings around the state. It would take pressure off of the engineers and he suggested correctly that I knew as well as any of them what we did and how we could do it. It didn't mean longer hours and other than more travel than I usually am accustomed to, the adjustment was seamless. That Thursday I was scheduled for a meeting with a big state college that was planning a huge addition to their athletic complex including a brand new state of the art, all weather practice facility usable by all major sports teams all year round. That was part of the reason I thought it would be a perfect day for my revenge showcase for Hank and boy was I ever right.

I went a little on the sexy side for my business meeting attire that day with a stylish business suit that included a skirt instead of pants. The skirt stopped a little before it probably should have, revealing quite a bit of my lower thigh and my stockings. Bright red ruffles of a blouse poked out around my chest that cut almost low enough to show cleavage but not quite, serving as a kind of tease to any who were looking my way and there were plenty. My hair was perfect before I got out of the car but the wind didn't harm it too badly on the way across the campus. All in all I looked damn good and walked like I knew it. The college guys noticed.

I'm certainly not a feminist of any type but I felt like a powerful force of energy and sexuality walking across towards the meeting that day. There was parking closer to the building where the meeting was being held but I wanted to walk across more campus and passed more guys, college guys, young adult studs who were hungry for an experienced, powerful and sexy woman. I showcased everything I thought the hot guys would be attracted to as I strutted across towards the meeting, at least I showcased as much as I could without looking like a slut.

It started to appear that I wouldn't get any direct interaction with anyone before I was scheduled to be talking to a room full of old men who smelled like aftershave and thought way too highly of their ability to flirt when a basketball rolled in front of me. I glanced down at the ball and then over in the direction it had come from and saw an entire team of jocks looking at me. Half of them turned away the moment I glared at them and a few more kept staring but not in the way I wanted. One guy looked at me in a different way than the others with confidence in his eyes. He jogged over towards me with an easy smile on his handsome face.

As he came to a stop I had already seen that he was well over six feet tall, probably a starter on the basketball team from the looks of things. Looking down at me he smirked and said, "Sorry about that miss. I guess the pass got away from me." I knew from the confident look in his eyes and the knowing smile that the pass had gone exactly where he wanted it to go.

"Really?" I bent over and picked the ball up then handed it to him with a knowing stare of my own, "You should keep a better hold on your balls young man." Bringing my finger to my lips in a shushing motion I whispered, "Unless you need someone to show you how."

His eyes bugged out for a split second, the surprised look quickly replaced by his confident smile. I asked him how long he would be practicing and he said for a good thirty minutes before hitting the showers. In a suggestive way I mentioned how far I parked away from the building and hinted that I might need someone to walk me safely to my car if any studs like him were still around when the meeting was over. He nodded and said that he thought he knew someone who could get me to safety and then jogged back to his game. I watched him go, wondering at once if I was crazy or daring or both.

After that it was on to business and the meeting went pretty much like most such meetings go. The college planned to build this many buildings and renovate that many more over the course of a ton of year and wanted input from all of their partners on what kind of budget space each needed. There was of course no way to know until the specific projects were divided out and plans drawn up but my boss knew they would ask such questions because they usually did, so I had a rough number I was allowed to let them have. I gave our rough estimate with a few points of interest, making it sound like I knew what I was doing the entire time. From there it went around the table with all doing pretty much the same thing. From that point the meeting consisted of a bunch of usual talking and I had to remind myself that my boss would want to see my notes to keep myself from writing yada yada blah blah or drawing pretty pictures on the paper.

Within a few minutes of the meeting ending I had mixed up conversation with the others and sufficiently rubbed shoulders with the right people so that I could excuse myself. Honestly I didn't expect anyone to be waiting out there other than maybe a few practicing late. The meeting had gone on a little longer than I thought it would and I knew the tall and handsome hunk I had flirted with would be long gone. It was probably for the best, I told myself. What was I really expecting to happen between someone my age – however great of shape I'm in – and a young college jock like that? I was kidding myself, surely.

"Walk a lady to her car?"

The voice was brooding and somewhat familiar. But it couldn't be. It wouldn't be him. I turned towards the greeting and saw him standing there all cleaned up. He was wearing jeans that looked old but were probably not, a tight t-shirt and a baseball cap with his letter jacket dangling over his right shoulder. Damn if he didn't wait for me. Butterflies began to fly around in my stomach and I felt supremely nervous for the first time since I can remember. "Huh?"

He walked over towards me with a smile that seemed much more inviting and sweet than I figured him for when I flirted before, "I don't want you to feel threatened by anyone on this campus on the way across to your car ma'am. Are you going towards the clock tower?" He pointed roughly in the direction of my car.

I didn't know quite what to say until I heard voices behind me of the older men who I had just met with, some of which were likely his coaches and certainly the Dean was among them. A smile crept towards the side of my mouth and I nodded, "I surely am. It'd be great if you would walk me in that direction. Thank you so much."

"No problem," he began to walk a comfortable distance ahead and to the side of me as we began to make our way in that direction.

I couldn't quite get a fix on what his intentions were. Earlier I was certain he wanted to mix up something blessedly wrong with this sexy older woman but now he genuinely seemed to want only to walk me to the car. Maybe he was only playing up for the guys in the meeting but he seemed to really want to stay a safe distance away from me. As we turned one final corner passed the long closed building that they apparently called the clock tower because of the old clock on top of it, I began to understand that he was really only going to walk me to my car. I'd been fooling myself after all.

"The clock tower has been closed for a few months now as they rework parts of it," he said with a point in that direction before slowing down. "It's not all that creepy for a closed building though."

"No?" I said flippantly.

"Nope," he said and suddenly grabbed my shoulder and spun me over towards the side wall. He lightly allowed me to rest against the brick wall and nodded towards the building, "Want to see the inside or do you really only want me to walk you to the car?"

Once again he had taken me by surprise and I didn't know quite what to say, at least not with my mouth. My eyes were another story altogether. I glared at him in want and desire. He was experienced enough at least to know what that look in my eyes meant. Quickly he took me by the shoulders and then let his hand slip to my wrist as he opened the door and led me inside. Apparently they didn't bother locking the side door or the students were the only ones who knew it was open. He led me into the darkened room and a little excitement began to creep towards uneasiness. It only served to increase my desire for the big stud pulling me towards a chosen spot.

He finally stopped and led me against the inside wall where he quickly took his shirt off and reached for my suit jacket then unbuttoned it and jerked it quickly off of my shoulders. It fell to the floor and he then removed his pants and revealed a large shaft that was standing eagerly out towards me, fully erect. I have expected him to ask me if this is what I wanted but he didn't stop, only reached to quickly unbutton my blouse and broke a few buttons off as he finally jerked it open. He pulled my bra down and squeezed my breasts before wrapping his lips around my nipple.

The pace was set quickly as he unzipped and lowered my skirt but didn't even bother taking down my panties. He only lifted me into his arms and moved the fabric of my panties to the side as I wrapped my hands around his neck. His cock slammed into me, shoving its way deep inside of me the first time and even deeper the second time he thrust it inside. My head rocked back as he waited no time at all before slamming into my hips harder and harder. I'd never had anyone enter me that hard and that fast with that much passion before and it was driving me crazy.

He knew just what he was doing as he worked over my breasts with one hand while the other rested on my butt as he rammed me so rough that I already felt my butt cheeks getting pink with the constant slap of his hips to mine. Over and over he rocked my body and I felt the first orgasm building very quickly. Just when he pinched my nipple hard I felt my climax wash over me, making him shudder and groan in pleasure.

The path for his hungry cock was even easier then as he lowered me to the floor and turned me around. I bent over and braced my hands against the wall as he pulled my panties out and I heard the thin lace fabric rip as he forcefully jerked them off of me. His hand grabbed a fist of my hair and jerked me hard back into him from behind. It felt so unbelievable that I wanted it to go on forever but I knew the pace he had set was not one for a long encounter. It didn't matter because a second orgasm rammed over my ravished body as he began moaning that he was close.

I was ready right then but he somehow held off for longer. By the time another few minutes passed, I felt the sting of his hips slamming into mine in concert with the wanting pleasure he filled me with. The big jock was claiming my pussy with the words he was groaning out, just like you'd expect a young jock to do in the throes of passion. I didn't mind one bit, actually wanted to give it to him willingly for another hour or two if possible.

Finally he pulled out and I turned around as I dropped to my knees. His hand was wrapped around his big throbbing cock as I grabbed it between my lips and took a massive load into my mouth. It was so much that I gagged a little bit before recovering and swallowing all but a little that was dripping down my chin. I wiped it with my finger and licked it off as I stood up and glared at him.

He was clearly spent and bending over at the waist, "Oh, my god, that was fucking amazing! I don't even know your name but..."

I put a finger to his lips as he stood up, "Shh... don't bother with names." I pulled my clothing back on as I spoke, "That really was something else. Are you going to walk me to my car now?"

It looked like he could barely walk after what he had just done to me and I felt the effects of the rough encounter as well but hid it well. We walked quietly to the car and then he said, "I practice there every day for the next four months and then again in the fall. Lady, you find yourself on campus..."

I smiled and cut him off, "Who knows? Maybe we'll meet again one day. Thank you for keeping me safe on the way to my car. Bye now."

That was it. Hank could tell something had happened by the way I acted over the next few days and I didn't hold back when I told him what I had done and asked him how it felt. He didn't like it then and still doesn't now but it has at least started a new conversation between us. Whether things will work out between us long-term is up in the air but if we do work it out and figure out a new normal for the two of us, I think I know a few terms Hank will have to meet first.

PARIS MOOD SWING

Kat spent the whole drive to the beach in a pissy mood. Initially, Derek thought it was something he had done to upset her," how can you come to Paris only for you to be angry instead of catching all the fun available" but when her snide comments continued while they were looking for a decent place to set up, he realized that she was in an unusual mood When she did he wouldn't still be with her, she didn't get them much, but when she did she was insufferable.

Between the cloudy sky, which was still threatening to rain given the prediction and the 20-minute walk from the parking lot, they were able to find a place where not many cars were around. "I didn't know Paris has this type of weather" I said and at that's when Kat announced that she was going for a swim while he set it all up. She took off her t-shirt and shorts and unveiled her new bikini. As she purchased it last week, he'd seen it, the thin bows keeping the bottom together made it a bit more daring than her standard wardrobe, but who was he to tell her how to dress? She flung his clothing over him and ran away. As Derek set up the chairs and the umbrella he decided enough was enough, and this childish behavior would end.

As Kat returned to his chair 15 minutes later Derek was reading his book. "I thought you'd join me, what the hell?" she told him.

He looked up at her and he turned his frustration to genuine anger. She stood in front of him, wrapped her long blond hair in a ponytail hanging over her shoulder's top. Water dropped down her ample arms, where her white bikini material not only carefully covered her curves, but had become nearly translucent. Her dark red pussy is visible through the costume, her nipples still firm from the cold water of the ocean.

"Kat, do you think that's fair?" he urgently demanded.

"What?" she replied in frustration.

"You're moaning all the way up here, from how miserable you are to how horrible

I've been walking, then you're leaving me to do all the setup and now this!" he found out.

"Derek, relax." she cast him off.

"Don't tell me to relax, you've been acting like a kid all day. Practically asking for a spanking" And her mood shifted with the word spanking. She knew he was dangerous and deadly. He had previously spanked her because she behaved in a selfish way. It wasn't something that he often did, but in the 10 months that they had been dating, he had done it more than once. She knew some time later, she had deserved it.

"You're right, I'm sorry. I'm going to start behaving better," she said, "I think I'm right, I don't need you to remind me, just as I don't need you to be so immature.

"Just no. At least not here, I'm going to behave for the rest of the day and you can still threaten me when we get home." It was not a question that was unfair. He had never before spanked her in public and that definitely crossed a line. But one seemingly about to be crossed especially In a place where memories can linger a long time for both of us.

"If it was just a matter of you being rude on the trip, I might have entertained that alternative, but I think we both know that your bathing suit is too much to overlook, and you're going to be spanked. There weren't many people in sight, and there was no one really close, but there were people who would see what they did. Testimonies of spanking a grown woman on her bottom, Just thinking about it was humiliating.

"Now," he insisted.

Kat surrendered to her fate, then smiled. She laid down on his shoulder. The bikini bottoms were close, and it met him invitingly in the round of her butt. She was in great form, and her ass looked incredible.

"I don't want to do this, but we know that you both need it," he said.

He replied "Indeed, sir. He swats her right cheek. There was a loud, wet slap noise and in sudden pain she screamed out. It was more robust than any of them would have anticipated. The wet material seemed to have heightened both noise and pain. He changed his power, checking her right cheek while swatting. Again, she yelled at the pain, but not nearly so much. "Well done." he asked her. She said there is nothing, as her left cheek began to turn red through to the sheer material.

"I think you're going to do ten more for your disrespectful attitude," he continued, "count them out and tell me you're sorry to be disrespectful."

"One. I'm sorry I was disrespectful," she said devotedly. Spank, she just got stuck in there. "Two. I'm sorry I've been disrespectful," she said, even if he doubted she meant that. Never ...... never. Spank. Spank. Spank. Spank. Down to left buttock.

"Uggh, Three, I'm sorry I was disrespectful." Her eyes started to water in her ass from the sting, but still her voice was almost emotionless.

Spank, hit swat back her right cheek.

"Muuh" she silently groaned "Three, I'm sorry I was rude." SPANK, the force of the blow intensified, causing her to kick her legs involuntarily.

"Hold on." She ordered. "And continue counting"

"Ffff, five. I'm sorry I was, I've been disrespectful," she said with gritted teeth.

SPANK YOU. He hit her ever-reddening rear end once again. She let out a grunt yet again.

A hundred yards or so away, Kat could see a few turns to look around. They may not have been able to see specifics, but they had to be able to see enough to realize that she was being spanked in public. She turned back, in embarrassment.

"Want to start right from the start?" Derek asked her.

"SIX." She blurred out, hoping he wouldn't restart desperately because she had lost her mind. "I'm so sorry I was rude." Smiled Derek. He realized she was just trying to avoid the extra swats but a nice touch was the "so sorry." Not that it would stop him from going any further.

SPANK YOU. That one was no harder than the last one, but the stinging started to build and heat burned her back.

"Seven. I'm sorry I was disrespectful," she replied this time quickly, but from her watering eyes her vision was blurry. Still, she maintained any emotional response.

Spank. Spank. Derek had actually lessened that blow's force, not really wanting to hurt her, but she couldn't feel the difference. Her left cheek was bright red, and not far behind the right. She was resisting tears but she could still guess what the pair are doing, or experience the sight to anyone else.

"Nine. I'm sorry I've been insensitive," she said through long, labored breaths. It hurt, but she wanted not to cry.

Derek shook his shoulder. When she was in the wrong she was always like this. They had a good relationship but sometimes she would get stubborn and fight tooth and nail to not have to admit that she had made a mistake. It wasn't attractive and wasn't something that he'd put up with. And that's where they were now, she held back tears, because to cry would be to admit defeat. The cry would look inside, and see a flaw. Crying would be a moment of honesty, when it would do most harm.

Spank. Spank. "No, no. I'm so sorry I've been, disrespectful," Derek was impressed. She sounded almost sincere, and sincere meant that she had learned a lesson which was the point of this. But it has not cut nearly.

SPANK YOU! It was the toughest yet. One of those it-got-worse-before-got-better kinda pains, she yelped in pain. "T-tu-ten. I'm sorry......" she breathed deeply. that I was rude." "I'm amazed. You've taken everything I think you can be like the mature adult." Derek assured her while he lovingly caressed her butt. He could sense the air radiating through the damp material from its edges.

Her breathing was laboured but returned to normal already.

"Thank you for making me realize that I was immature," she said. "I think it was necessary." "I'm happy you think so," he told her, as he kept rubbing her glorious but deeply red ass. "Because we're not done yet," she objected. "But you said five!"

"I said ten would do for your disrespectful behaviour." he told her. "But we still have to deal with your bikini." "My bikini?" "Yes. Did you know that when you wet it would become transparent, when you bought it?" he asked.

She wavered. Trying to figure out how great a risk lying would be. It was she who decided against it. Lying, whatever the punishment, would just make it worse.

"Yeah, I understood" muttered she.

"Well, I can not stop you if you want to show your body to strangers." he said. "I am not good at guessing but if I am to try, it wasn't about you feeling pretty or sexy or anything? It was an attempt to make me jealous, wasn't it?" It was immature and petty, but when she bought it that was exactly what she thought. She nodded slowly, hesitantly.

 "What was that, I am sorry?" he asked.

"Yeah, I was... I thought some guys would see and respond to me, and you... you would be jealous," she confessed. "It's not me at all respectful. Playing games rather than being part of an adult relationship," he said. "Did I ever treat you in this way?" he said.

"No sir" she answered.

"Ok, I guess the offence should be matched to retribution." he concluded. "The next round would be appropriate on a nude leg." "NO! PLEASE" she asked, looking about. The pair still stood there. And there was someone walking a dog down by the river. If he had yanked off her bikini she would be fully exposed to them. "Don't I?" he said.

"I mean, please sir," she promised, "I swear I'll behave."

"In the past I think you made that promise," he told her.

Slowly he pulled her bikini bottoms at a bow.

"Sir, please." she begged, almost crying.

The bow got undone, and he began tugging at the other one.

"You're the one who wanted to show off in public. It's just me that's helping you," he said.

She breathed hard, then regained composure. The bow came loose, and as he unwrapped a present, he removed her bikini bottoms. Her bare bottom looked breathtaking.

"No need to count this time, but I want to know what exactly you're sorry for after each fifth. Okay?" Each FIFTH ONE? She said, practically panicking. That meant that there would be at least another five, very likely more.

"Okay?" she replied, "Yes sir," knowing that complaining would ultimately only make it worse. So, to put it that way.

He stroked her bare ass for a moment, taking the time to dry her off using his towel. He was gentle, and felt good on her ass with the soft towel.

"Get ready." he admonished her. Spank, Spank, Spank, Spank, Spank-Spank. In quick succession, he swatted her. When he finished and waited she had barely reacted to the first one. She stared back over his shoulder, on him. Her eyes watered once more.

"I'm sorry, um, I've been trying to make you jealous. It's been immature with me," she admitted.

He grinned and said "thank you for accepting this." The other sets were slower Spank. Spank. Spank. Spank. Only chewing her lips

Spank. Spank. She closed her eyes, and battled the agony.

Spank. Spank. She moaned, and couldn't bear it any longer.

Spank. Spank. She kept crying and her ass pulled away from him. He shifted her back to Spank place. She crossed her legs and let out an "Aaahhhh" and tried to form words that she said "I am..." but had to pause. She had her eyes closed to hold in tears. He stroked her pussy until she could move on a minute later. "I'm sorry that I handled you so poorly on the drive up. Last night I had a bad night at work, but I shouldn't have taken it out on you." "Thank you. If you want to talk about it later, we should." he added.

The next round he took off. She was there, he sensed it and he wanted to finish this. Spank, spank. He struck her dead ass middle. The pain fired through her.

Spank. Spank. It caused her to groan harder but she kept fighting it.

SPANK YOU. She let out a whimper even harder and a few tears fell.

SPANK YOU! It was the hardest yet, and the dam burst with it. She started sobbing uncontrollably. She turned to look at him still lying across his lap. She spoke in sentence fragments, though the crying and sniffling he could scarcely understand. "Sorry... thank you... behaviour... fair to you" She kept caressing her ass she was crying. "You were a pretty bad girl," he told her. "But we're almost done." "O, O, Okay," she managed through her tears and didn't question him at all.

"Only one load more." he told her. He did not finish the last set technically, but this was not about a specific number of spanks, it was about learning a lesson from her.

Spank, he no longer swatted her as hard but they still stung something fierce. She just kept crying, Spank. She trembled like she was sobbing.

Spank. Spank. She was gasping for a Spank breath. She buried her hands in her face.

Spank. Spank. She sunk into his leg.

He reassured her once more, trying to touch her bottom, while shhh-shhhing softly. She slipped off his legs, pulling off some of the pressure from her butt. She looked up at him, wiping her arms and hands off the tears from her eyes.

"Thank you Derek. I'm sorry that I've done that. I promise that I'm going to be better," she said.

"I know you are going to," he told her.

She looked at his crotch, his shorts did nothing to conceal his massive erection. She reached into his jeans, to explore it.

"They want me to...?" she asked.

She will also fellate him, following a spanking. It wasn't something he expected, nor something he ever asked for. It was merely her way of both thanking him and letting him know she wasn't mad at him for doing what needed to be done. "Kat, this is not something you need to do here." She glanced around. In reality she had missed the last few minutes that they were outside. Everything had gone missing below her reddened heart. There was the couple still standing, stealing glances. Further down was the person walking the dog, somebody in the distance was flying a kite off.

"No. They've seen what you've done so they know I'm a bad girl. I need to show them that I can be a good girl too." There weren't so many people out there and whoever says no to a blowjob?

He just smiled. She reached up, pulling his hard cock out of the rock. She bent forward and licked out his shaft from the base, up to the top.

"I'll be a good girl." she told him. " Let me be a naughty girl. "She then gobbled his cock in her mouth." Fuck, Kat, "he said, flapping her head up his dick and down. There was no mistake what she was doing, even from speed. Her tongue was wet with saliva, she guzzled as she gradually pulled her length into her mouth.

"Oh god, you're such a good girl," he urged.

"Mmmfff?" she asked, staring at him, cock in her mouth warm.

"Kat, I'm not going to last long, ugh." She pulled his dick out of her ass.

"In my mouth." was all she said before plunging right back down on his dick, sucking and bobbing as quickly as she could. She also grabbed one side of his shaft, squeezing it as she sucked him. oh no such a fucking good girl" he said. He reached down, grabbing her head, pulling as deeply into her throat as he could go.

"Take it. Take the fucking cock." he ordered, and then burst into her mouth. She swallowed everything before getting his dick out of her mouth. She even gave it one last playful kiss on the head before he put it back in his shorts.

He told her: "Thank you, Kat."

"Thank you, Derek," she told him, waving behind her amid the flames. "I just did need that."

Safe Word

Raina had driven out of her dorm to this unknown part of town since she wanted to try out something fresh, but as soon as she stepped out from her vehicle, she reminded herself that although the entire weekend had been blocked out to this 'experience,' it was her idea and she would back out at any moment.

"Simply state the 'safe word' and everything finishes," she said.

As long as she'd known about sex, the shy, the pretty coed had experienced shameful sexual dreams. Alone in her room late at night, she dreamed of a faceless guy taking complete control of her, bringing out her hidden wants, tying her up, 'forcing' her to perform all of the nasty, naughty things she knew she'd adore ... but she was a wonderful girl with fine friends and a wonderful family, so she'd been ashamed to tell anyone about her secret needs.

Nobody on earth knew how badly she wanted to get fucked hard and filthy, just how her pussy dripped when she thought of a powerful man taking charge of her ... But she decided on her twenty-second birthday the time had come to find out what could happen if she really lived out her secret needs.

She was courageous a couple of minutes ago, secure inside her vehicle, but today, as she shut the door behind her and made her way down the darkened street, she'd been wondering if that was such a fantastic idea.

She tottered up the route on the way-too-high heels that the stranger had requested ... ordered ... her to wear, and she scanned the abandoned road nervously, worried that somebody would watch her make a fool of herself.

Raina had a fine curvy figure—ample breasts and large, round buttocks, but she wasn't the kind of woman to dress sexy. Therefore, it was difficult for her to visit the shop and purchase what the guy told her she needed to wear ... but here she was looking like an entire slut: A skin-tight black gown that only covered her bum cheeks, tiny thong panties without a bra, her round breasts bouncing with each step she took.

Her face flushed with humiliation as a motorist slowed down to look at her strutting down the block, however, she felt a rush of horniness when she imagined herself, her long, straight black hair dangling down her back, her breasts bounced as she got closer to the speech he'd given her.

She'd 'met' the stranger through the Internet among dating sites. She had taken a somewhat provocative advertisement, simply to see what would occur, and his reply jumped from the many guys desperate to fulfill her. Something about how he composed himself appealed to her for some unknown reason, and she couldn't hurry to call him quickly enough and organize the details of their assembly. Even as he told her exactly what her 'missions' were (what she had been to wear, what she had been to bring with her for their date, etc), she barely believed she'd consented, but she was walking down the road, carrying a bag filled with gear and also dressed like a streetwalker.

She swallowed hard and knocked on his doorway. No response, however, the door slowly swung open. The area was dim, moodily lit using a reddish light. She stood in the door.

"Come in," a voice from the shadows said gently, and she stepped across the brink. "Step into the middle of this room, disperse the contents of this bag outside alongside you, and get on your knees and hands ... Today!"

For some reason she didn't even come close comprehension, Raina failed at it. She stepped into the darkened room, dumped the bag of leather straps, blindfolds, sex toys and handcuffs alongside her, then with a burning face—her heart pounding and hands shaking—she knelt on the carpeted floor, hands in front of her.

"That's great," the voice stated.

And she appeared like this, fear mixed with enthusiasm, every nerve end pulsing, before, finally, after what seemed like forever, she heard faint footsteps behind her.

She felt his presence in the room. She felt a heavy hand caress her buttocks through her dress. She turned her head to look at him.

SLAP!

He brought down his hands down to her buttocks, along with stinging fire.

"Keep your eyes down, slut," he shouted, and her mind snapped. She sensed him roll her skin-tight dress up along her thighs, over her buttocks, and noticed his breath speeding up as he caressed her round butt.

This is mad, she believed to herself, but she didn't catch up. She didn't say the word they'd agreed to ahead, she simply knelt there, panting softly as a stranger felt her bum.

He roughly grabbed her lips. She couldn't help but moan as she fell obediently to the ground. He caressed her round buttocks, hefted its weight, then proceeded down onto her thighs, tickling her inner thighs with the back of his hands softly as he knelt behind her, his palms edging nearer to her swollen cunt.

She was half-conscious. Moaning somewhat when he eventually touched her glistening pussy through her lace panties, she melted into his hands as he squeezed her crotch wantonly against him. He grabbed a fistful of her hair and pulled back her head, whispering hoarsely in her ear, "You like this, don't you?"

She felt his hard, bare torso on her back and shivered.

"Tell me you like it," he hissed.

"I enjoy it ..."

"You like what?"

"I-I-I like you touching my pussy," she confessed, then moaned loudly.

This was what she'd always wanted: Someone to discharge her inner slut.

He laughed softly as he continued to rub her wet pussy through her panties, then reached out to catch one her dangling breasts along with his opposite hand while leaning his weight against her and whispering in her ear.

"That's it," he mumbled, "get yourself off my hands, slut."

She ground her pussy into his hands while moaning even louder. She'd never been so sexy in her entire life. She panted and moaned while grinding her stiff little clit against his hands ... she wished to please him so badly; she churned wildly on his hands, thrusting her hips around in circles because he stroked her hair and back.

A low growl escaped her lips and her muscles tightened ...

"Oh ... fuck ..." she uttered as a gigantic orgasm shook through her entire body, causing her to convulse again and again.

Her arms and legs shook as her earthquake subsided and she returned to the planet ...

'Oh my God, thank you so much ..." she cried, hoping their dream game to be over soon ... but he stopped her with a different hard slap to her buttocks and she felt the stinging feeling spread throughout her bum.

"Now, stand up."

She snapped to attention on shaky legs and got her first look at the stranger. He stood in the dim light, shirtless, but wearing black jeans with a riding crop in hand, a serious look on his face. The stranger was about six feet tall with short brown hair, piercing blue eyes and a sculpted torso.

He wasn't bad in any way. She stole a fast glance at his crotch and was pleased to realize the scene clearly turned him on too: his huge cock was ramming the denim and pushed against his thigh.

"Get naked for me. Now!"

She lifted her slutty dress over her head and bent down to take her panties off, making the cloth fall on the ground as she faced him. She stood still, naked and blushing.

"We're going to have a great deal of pleasure ..." he said gently while stroking his hard dick through his trousers. "Get over here and take off my jeans."

She promptly knelt before him and undid his belt buckle.

His hands were within her hair as she zipped down his fly. She gasped at the size of his penis that flopped out ... it was half-hard, and it was the biggest dick she'd ever seen. He stepped over her panties and grabbed his dick from the base, pumping it a couple of times before her lips ...

"Oooh, I can't wait to cum around your face," he said.

She felt himself blushing, turned on by how primitive that he'd been, therefore distinct from the 'fine' boys she was used to.

"In actuality, that's exactly what I am going to perform ... you just kneel there, slut, although I'll jerk off all over your face," he stated, his fist-raising the rhythm on his dick.

"Lick my balls while I jerk off," he commanded.

She did. She got right between his thighs and started tonguing his thick bag while he stroked his dick, sometimes stopping to lick at it on her delicate cheek.

She felt her pussy growing wet and moved her hands down to perform on her clit.

"Open up," he panted, and she did.

He put the head of his large cock inside her mouth and slowly slid it backward. Her lips bulged, but she started as wide as she could and took the head of his dick into her mouth while he continued to jack off.

Spit dribbled down her face as she furiously tongued his tough slab while working her pussy.

"Mmmm ... God ... yessss ..." he panted and started fucking her face harder.

She felt his penis slide out of her lips and hot jets of cum shot into her face, starling her. Spurt after spurt of hot goo coated her panting face and dripped down her breasts.

She'd been crazed with sex and licked every drop of semen off her lips while her own orgasm tore through her.

He stood still and looked at her, dazed ... seeing her swallow all the cum ...

'Don't overlook any," he breathed as she scooped it off her breasts and into her mouth.

"You and I will have a lot of pleasure this weekend," he said, eyeing the bondage equipment she'd brought along with her.

Raina could just imagine.

City of Desire

I'm not what you'd call a fantastic woman. I quickly found that I enjoyed sex after creating the type of curvy body which made guys want to have sex with me. I am by no means a perfect ten. I'm cuter than sexy, but I have an above-average bra size, thick lips that are always wrapped around a tough cock and I have a willingness to spread my thighs.

Some folks would call me simple. Others could call me a slut. I'm not denying being either. Most of the things they say about me are accurate. Yes I've sucked my fair share of cocks, been fucked by my fair share of guys and even let some of them splatter their hot cum all over my skin.

However, I'd been on a one on one basis every time. Some of these may have been one night stands, a number of them may have had girlfriends, but the number of individuals involved consistently remained at two. Yet I will admit—or nearly admit as long as I've had sex—I've played around with the dream of having sex with more than one man at the same time.

It'd never be just a dream. I mean what type of woman would do this type of thing? What type of slut would allow guys to fuck her like this? Just considering it flipped my lacy thong into a wet mess.

I believe my first experience with the notion of a gangbang arrived in the kind of reading my dad's dirty magazines. The very first time I responded with disgust, however, the second time I found myself at home and took the stash out, then began flipping through them. I wished to be the woman from the centerfold. I wished to be like the girls I discovered from the tales in the trunk. Girls that had sexual sex, much more enjoyable than my awkward and unsatisfying sex life at the moment. The story that stood out for me was based around a girl who went camping with her husband. They bunch made a couple of friends and one thing led to another with five guys fucking her, filling her with cum.

The following experience came in the shape of a porn movie among my immature man friends who'd put on during a party. In the lady's bleached blonde hair to her giant fake tits, everything about it dropped into the class of fake. Certainly not a turn on like the aforementioned narrative, but seeing her take on four giant cocks somehow made the dream a little more genuine.

The most recent experience with the concept of a gangbang came not too long after my own graduation. Really right after. That night everybody gathered for celebrations, a crazy night for certain but I don't think anybody needed a wilder night compared to my friend Becky. At one of those parties she ended up sucking off half a dozen men and fucking four of them. As soon as I heard the story I responded with disgust, but deep down inside me, I wished that it'd been me.

But I did not want the entire town knowing I'd allowed a bunch of guys to bang me. Becoming simple or a slut is something you'd be able to write off as being youthful. Obtaining a gangbang follows you about. You'll visit the grocery store and a person will recognize you as that chick that let four guys fuck you.

However, I couldn't stop thinking about the dream. It was the dream I believed about late at night once I found myself alone in my area without a man to phone over. An enjoyable dream, but nothing I would ever make become a reality. Or so I thought.

"I thought it would only be a girls' weekend," I started when Ashley put down her mobile phone. Following a messy breakup, I wasn't in the mood to take care of any member of the male species.

"I understand, but I didn't believe Tyler would be in the city."

She looked at me, then took a sip of her vodka and cranberry. We'd been home sitting at her aunt's beach condo and put a significant dent in her liquor. I wasn't certain how she intended to conceal that, but she didn't appear to be overly worried.

"What do you really need me to perform? Tell him he can't come over? That will go down nicely. I'm sorry."

"I'm so sorry, I'm in this crabby mood," I muttered.

"They will only be here for a little while, then they're heading out to town."

"Who is they?"

While I debated the severe ideas about not dating, Tyler did possess some appealing buddies; older, more mature, sexy college men. Perhaps I could hold off the relationship vow of silence for now.

"I'm not sure. He said 'we' while we were on the telephone. He didn't mention who was included."

I expected it comprised of James. James, while he wasn't the school quarterback, seemed like he could've been using a well-built figure and was a man next door with great looks.

"Just how long are they likely to be here?" I asked.

"He didn't say."

"Damn you," I stated with a grin as the funk encompassing me began to lighten up.

I hurried to my bedroom and dug through my purse. We spent all afternoon on the shore, and after a hot shower, I wore a set of old football shorts and a raggedy tank top. Not precisely the type of clothing I'd considered the dress to impress collection. I didn't pack much, but I made the mistake of packaging more bikinis than real clothes. I discovered a more straightforward tank top, a set of jean shorts and washed underwear, just in case.

I quickly brushed my hair, put on some makeup and managed to put on the shorts as the doorbell rang.

Since Ashley opened the door, I peeked through my bedroom door. Tyler came in with a case of beer and a kiss for Ashley. James followed closely and I stepped into the hallway with a grin. He seemed just like what I'd have over my commanding, nevertheless cheating ex-boyfriend. Then two guys came in who were equally new to me. I started wondering just who my doctor prescribed for me.

Tyler introduced them to Devon and Rick. Devon looked like the poor boy my mother would despise, finished with tattoos all over him and rugged, jet black hair. Rick appeared more like a man I could really see myself in a relationship. I narrowed down my choices to James and Devon.

The initial plan had them only sticking around to get some drinks before going Downtown to a few pubs. Initially, I didn't really enjoy that program, however, after a couple of drinks, I changed my mind. They immediately reminded me why I'd been pissed off at the male members of the species. They hit on me and stared at my tits to the stage it became uneasy. I'll admit in the beginning I enjoyed the focus. It felt great to be reminded there were other guys on the market, but it quickly became more than that. I wished to cope with this particular weekend. I'd been glad Ashley was outside on the balcony and they would be departing shortly.

"I will be right back. Do you need anything?" Ashley asked as she slid open the sliding glass door.

"Another drink?" I'd been pacing myself, but they left me wanting to consume more.

"You have it?"

I believed she'd be back following a couple of minutes. How long could a stop in the restroom along with a boil at the kitchen take? I didn't have a third eye, but it looked like it took far longer than it should've taken. After Devon undressed me with his eyes for the third time in a moment, I decided to take things into my own hands for my beverage.

Since I opened the sliding glass door, I recognized Tyler had gone missing from the balcony. I feared the worst and my fears were confirmed when I saw that Ashley's white bedroom door was shut.

I didn't know what to do besides getting another beverage. I just didn't need to return on the porch, but the condominium didn't leave any other place else to conceal myself. Before I could make a decision the three of them joined me in the kitchen.

They included me in the conversation about shores, but I hardly took part in the other than nodding my head. My mind told me they were unattractive, but I understood they needed me. I'd be lying if I said I didn't need every one of them.

I sensed my body temperature increasing and I couldn't be certain if it was due to those three sexy men facing me, the air conditioning, or that I couldn't maintain myself at all. I envisioned being in bed with James. Sex with him could be a satisfying exercise. Devon would love to do something kinky, pushing me beyond what I felt comfortable doing. Rick would go out of the way to be certain he fulfilled me until he arrived.

All three of these had solid points, but I couldn't just grab them by the arms and drag them to the bedroom. Okay, maybe I really could, but it would be quite embarrassing for the other two.

My second thought wished I could blame the alcohol, nevertheless, I hardly needed a hot buzz. I pictured myself in bed with all three of them spread out around me, all of them nude, rock hard and ready for me. The idea left my cotton panties moist.

As they talked about fishing I completely stopped listening. What could it actually be like to own all three of these guys? Would I like it if they used me? Thinking these thoughts made me squirm from the counter. I took a long sip of my brightly colored, blended beverage and expected none of them had found my delight.

How can I do it? Can I just tell them I was miserable and wanted to get fucked?

The excitement in my body grew and my heart began to pound.

How would they respond? Imagine if I simply invited them to accompany me to the bedroom? Or could I simply drop to my knees on the kitchen tile?

I probably could've dropped to my knees since Ashley totally abandoned me. The next time two people were lonely, I intended to mention a couple of things to her. However, I didn't know how long they'd be. They'd not seen each other for a couple of weeks and probably needed to compensate for lost time. Part of the reason why I didn't want to encounter Tyler was due to their relationship. They'd been a happy couple that couldn't get enough of each other. Ashley and I were only eighteen, but I could see both of them getting married.

I didn't have a problem finding men. So far, however, after a couple of things always became dull to find or I found other reasons to finish the relationship. I wasn't prepared to repay, but I knew there was more than only one night stands and flings. Yet every one of them stood around me. I didn't need a relationship. I wanted to get fucked.

What would Ashley say if she came out and watched me hanging over the sofa and they were lining up to fuck me? What would she say following morning when she came outside and found us lost with my bedroom door shut?

She understood about my flings and about my one night stands. But she didn't understand about this dream.

I could feel the blood flood through my veins. My panties clung into my wetness. It might either remain as a dream or it may turn into a reality.

I took a long sip of my drink, nevertheless barely buzzed. I took a deep breath. I leaned back from the counter and pushed my chest out. "Guys, I'm really fucking horny."

The conversation stopped mid-sentence. All three of them turned to look at me and their mouths dropped.

"What do you really wish to do about it?" Devon said, immediately recovering from the surprise, coming back to his old self.

"I wish to get fucked." I couldn't think that the words had come from out of my mouth.

"I would be pleased to assist you with that." He stepped towards me.

I put my hands up to stop him. "From all three of you."

I have said some slutty things, but nothing could ever top that.

The three of them looked at each other. It didn't feel real. I walked between Devon and James towards my bedroom. My bare feet touched the tile, then the carpet since I moved in my room, but it felt like walking on air.

They followed me into my room with James being the last to enter. I looked at him and he closed the door. For some reason the ornaments on the walls were all shore and nautical items such as seashells along with a compass which seemed like it would burst into a classic vessel. I didn't think of anything for a few minutes. Time stood still and they looked like predators about to strike their prey. I felt like a slice of meat and I grinned.

They stepped forward and I stepped back, then dropped onto the mattress. This was the mattress where it would occur where my dream would become a reality.

It began with palms. I felt a set of hands-on the buttons of my shorts. I felt another set of hands disturb my tank shirt. I looked up and watched Devon between my thighs along with Rick's hands pulling up my tank shirt to reveal my orange bra.

I wished I'd thought to wear a matching bra and underwear, but I didn't believe that mattered to them. Everyone looked at me, their eyes full of lust. A massive bulge formed within Devon's jeans.

My shorts came off and my purple underwear followed. A brand new set of palms joined in. I watched James set his hands between my thighs and felt his hands brush across my lips. I let out a soft moan. He told me to be silent, that I didn't want Ashley to listen, but I knew one way or the other she'd learn about this. He slipped a finger into me and rubbed his thumb across my sensitive clit. My tender moan became loud. I held my tongue as a last-ditch attempt.

A couple of moments after my tits were outside the cups of my bra. They didn't even bother to remove my tank top or bra all the way down. Rick's mouth found my nipple and I let out a shout as he bit it. His palms weren't as gentle as his mouth. I typically hated, really despised when guys went for my tits, but this time it turned me on.

When Rick took my nipple out of his mouth, he continued sucking on it. I watched Devon again as he stood between my thighs with his trousers and boxers down at his knees, directing his rock hard cock towards me moist center.

I understood then that I hadn't mentioned condoms. Following the breakup, I didn't believe I'd be needing them for some time, so I didn't keep any stashed away somewhere. I was on the pill instead, and unprotected sex wasn't brand new to me, but these three men were people I hardly knew. I understand that should've freaked me out, but it only turned me on more. I wanted to feel them inside me, leaving nothing to divide us. I wanted them all to cum inside me.

I stared at my legs and observed as Devon stepped ahead. Time seemed to slow down as I felt his penis touch my moist lips. It felt as though I could feel every cell of him merge with my own. It made my entire body twist with delight. He pushed into me and time returned to normal.

My wetness enabled him to easily push into me. He filled me, giving my whole body a sense of passion as I'd never felt before. There was no turning back now.

He grabbed my buttocks. I wrapped my palms around him for comfort as he started to thrust into me. I bit my lip, but I couldn't curb my moans.

He fucked me for a moment or two, but until he came anywhere near to a climax, he resigned. Before I knew what was happening, I felt the following cock enter me. I looked up and saw James. My dream would come true. With him and two other men, this is something I wouldn't forget. I'll admit there could've been a single night where I had sex with my boyfriend at that time and churn out after that night to meet up with a different man. I'd thought of this as among the sluttiest of things I'd done, but it didn't even compare.

His thrusts got harder as everyone started to breathe harder. It was better than the exercise I'd imagined. He filled me with joy.

Right as I began to completely love it, he resigned. I found Rick coming up next. All three of these guys must've been talking, but I didn't recall any noise other than the hum of the air conditioner, the squeaking of the metallic framework and my extremities.

Devon and James left me to whine about the size department, however, Rick stood vertical and markedly bigger. He pushed into me and I could feel myself stretching to adopt him. I raised my grasp on the duvet as he began to thrust into me.

It wasn't a dream anymore. It was nowhere close to that now, but three guys were fucking me precisely at the same time. I was gangbanging. I wasn't the run of the mill slut anymore.

I wanted more. When James pulled out, I flipped over and stayed on my hands and knees. I didn't have to mention anything else. Someone took me from behind. I didn't know who it was initially until I looked back and watched Devon thrust. Rick came to my entrance. He knelt on his knees and put his penis near my mouth.

I licked his swollen head, tasting a hint of his salty precum. I opened my mouth and took him between my lips. I took him deep into my mouth while another guy fucked me. It didn't seem real. I sensed another set of hands-on my waist. Rick started fucking my mouth., using my mouth as my pussy. They used me for their pleasure and I adored it.

At some stage the enjoyment of a penis inside me, the sensation of a cock sliding between my lips and a set of hands me, made me drop. The delight overwhelmed my body. I closed my eyes and the orgasm erupted inside me used a huge force I'd never felt before. I didn't understand who I had in my mouth. I didn't know who'd been fucking me. The sensation sent me into a completely different world of enjoyment.

My orgasm was linked with another. I felt two controlled thrusts and in the last minute he pulled from me. I heard a grunt and understood that it'd been James behind me. Moments later I felt cum splatter onto my back. The hot, thick cum struck me so hard it nearly made me jump. He covered my butt with his cum.

Devon grabbed my head and pushed his cock down my throat. I didn't gag after as his succulent cum flooded my mouth. After he pulled back, I swallowed everything whole.

I wasn't done yet. I desired Rick. I desired his massive cock to satisfy me with his cum. I flipped myself over while the other two started putting their clothes back on. Rick nevertheless was nude from the waist down, his big cock still prepared for me.

He pushed me to the middle of the mattress and joined me. He climbed on top and took me. He didn't start off slow this time. He slammed his cock into me with everything he had. I moaned and cried out as his joy stuffed me, fucking me as though I was his slut.

I ended up together with him and rode him since it felt like the final cock I would get. I didn't just sit there. My entire body bounced up and down on his penis. I did what I could, shifting my entire body before he eventually gave me exactly what I desired.

As a powerful orgasm stuffed me, as my body began to stiffen while I arched my back, he pushed and unleashed a torrent of cum. My body shook into a blissful orgasm.

He rolled me off him after he was spent. I wasn't his girlfriend. I'd been some slut he and his friends had only fucked. They left me, my entire body sore and tired, drenched with sweat and cum still clinging to me. I could feel his cock throbbing inside me once I heard the front door open, then shut. I could taste the cum in my mouth. They fucked me, they used me. And I loved it. I felt dirty, I felt like a slut, I felt alive.

A couple of minutes after I heard a soft knock on my door. "Kayla?" Ashley asked.

"Yeah?" I said, getting up and donning a bathrobe.

"Could I come in?"

"Come."

"Are you OK?" Her face had a look of concern.

"Yeah." I couldn't hide my smile. I felt like I was shining.

"What happened?"

"Should I tell you?"

"And you're fine with it?"

"Yeah."

"You're such a slut."

We both giggled.

"I can't disagree with this."

"I never believed you'd do something like this. How can it be?"

"Words can't explain it."

I handed her the box score outline. Her mouth fell as I told how one man took me from behind while the other stuffed my mouth. Nevertheless, I think I saw a portion of her wanting to do it.

Sex Partner

." .. After you've done blowing Steve and John ... "Paige asked breathlessly," did you meet both guys again ... at the same time?

"Oh , yes, boy ... I took both of them ... at the same time ... a DP," I whispered.

Paige moaned and wiggled around in bed, "Oh gawd Jen, how could you?" I could never do anything like that ... I could never take two men at the same time.

"It was so good .... I loved it, and so did it. I want you to feel that. Are you going to fuck my guys with me, "I asked, nibbling at her ear?

Her mouth fell open and she inhaled drifting into the fantasy. She pulled her nightshirt over her breasts and twisted her panties to the side, freeing her swollen clit. She started fingering herself. I jiggled one of her freed tits and put it in my mouth for a moment, and then I licked her neck and back to her cheek and ear.

"Baby," I said, "you have to relax; and then trust; and then submit. It's heaven. Give yourself to it. Return to pleasure. You can take a man in your ass and your pussy at the same time. Imagine two men pleasing to you while they worship you."

She turned and licked at my lips, and I opened up, and for a few seconds we held our tongue closed. "Jen, we've got to stop now. It's too late. What if one of those bitches hears us? I've got to get going."

I was the Paige alarm clock. I will kiss and cuddle her up every morning. I've always made sure she woke up slightly. Our arms and legs will slowly intertwine in a small twin bed. It was during this time that I would share my personal misadventures, too. Our passion is going to grow. We were two sisters who shared sweet little secrets.

We've been quiet for a moment, thinking about our day ahead. Neither of us was able to get up there. Paige was fingering her nipples lightly. Instead she shaved her breasts. "Jen could you just ... just kiss my boobies ... just my boobies ... just for a little while? Pleeease? And then I really have to go to work"

Her thick auburn hair fell off the bed and flew to the floor. I raised myself above her long lean body and gradually stepped down on her tiny little tits. I gave every of them the love they deserved.

Her strawberry nipples were so sensitive that I barely had to touch them to increase her breathing and moaning. I knew her right now. She needed me to be very sweet. I'm never going to bite or suck too hard. I would open my mouth wide and suck in as much of her boob as I could. Instead I would twirl my tongue around her nipple with much of her boob in my mouth. I should curl up and brace against the wall of our house, so that I could suck her tit and fuck her pussy at the same time. This was making her nuts. I will kindly finish with the lightest kiss on each boob before moving on to her swollen pussy.

Her eyes were nearly closed when I looked down on her. Mine has always been available. Paige was absolutely gorgeous, particularly in the early morning, with the sun filtering through the blinds. She was the most attractive girl in her sorority.

She had the face and body of a model in New York. Me, the face and body of a porn star in California. The rest of the sorority girls were jealous and scared that they would steal friends from their boys. She was dazzled unmercifully by the promise she made. I figured it was going to drop the thread. After that, I was the only one able to share a room with her.

Stupid bitches, man. This never occurred to them that I was going to fuck their guys to death even before Paige stole one.

I've been working my way slowly down her tight chest, and I've been pulling at her navel ring ever so slightly. Once I found her snatch, I licked and kissed her stomach and pelvic bones.

I was sucking softly on her clit. Paige embraced it, and then. "Oh, fuck no ... oh, Jen ... noo, oh, baaabee ...... not today ... not today," she begged softly. "I've got a mid-term tomorr ... Oh Jen, it's no ... don't ... they 're going to hear me cum."

Then she gave a quiet little cry.

Her pelvis started to rock and twist. I cut her butt with both hands and started to mess around her little bung hole while I was still eating her sweet pussy. She squeezed the back of my head and let go of it. The last bit of her let go of it.

Her lower half rose up in the air to reach me. She moaned and began to enjoy her own breasts. Ohh Jen ... it's so sweet. Ohh, ohh ... it's so sweet. You fuckin 'feed me so good. So, damn good ... So fuckin 'sweet, uh, gaawd, I love it so ...

She placed her hands over her face and waited for her orgasm to take hold of her. Her lower body clenched and shook. I kept my face to her pussy and gave her a tight butt.

For a few seconds, she settled down and started to sob quietly. Her hands never left her face. She curled into a fetal ball and faced the wall.

"You're so fuckin' good....it's so sweet and so bad," she said softly, "I'm a fucking lezbo, and I love it so much."

I wasn't going to let her get away with that, and she kept licking her curled ass and pussy from behind. She calmed down and soon began to accept my face and tongue, going deeper into her from behind. She 'd bend her upper leg open. I thought it was going to give me better access to her. She was a terrific athlete and moved so quickly that I didn't realise what was going on until she had the upper ha.

She flipped me over before I realised what was going on. She was now on top of me laughing, raising my arms above my head with our fingers intertwined.

She kissed me hard and said, "Okay, my little slut, it's all your fault that we're skipping college. My turn is on you little slut to devour you. And if you make any noise, I'm going to put a gym sock in your mouth.

It was a serious threat, she knew that I was a screamer.

"You dirty little slut," I whispered, licking at her nose.

She used her strength and length to lick and kiss me up and down my arms, my back, all over my face, without allowing me to move.

"Relax, trust and submit," she said. "Submit to me this time." And when I started wiggling around her kisses and licks, she was smoother, softer and more receptive.

I've always began and generally controlled. It was special for us, so it was great to have her take care of me.

She squeezed my breasts. "Your boobs are all mine," she said. "All mine and I will play with them as long as I want." She was fascinated by my big boobs, and I just loved her little ones. I held her head, and I stroked her hair as she suckled me. It was a gentle, quiet love.

I let her do whatever she wanted to do. But any time I began to moan too much, she 'd place her tits or fingers in my mouth.

"Be still and suck it," she muttered. For what felt like hours, she loved me. Wonderful, slow and gentle foreplay.

She was going to bring me up and then take it away. Rewarding and slowing down; rewarding and slowing down. I started pleading for her to let me cum and then she turned around and dropped her pussy in my face and started eating it.

This is how we finished each other in a 69. Two disgusting little cats licking each other's pussies clean.

After a few minutes of post-coital bliss, she came back to me at the head of the bed.

"You destroyed me, you know," she said.

"What do you mean by that," I asked.

"After this, I couldn't imagine you've been having missionary sex with the same man for thirty years. I can't believe what I'm saying, but I really want to join you with John and Steve, at least once to know what it's like."

We kissed and teased each other about the scent of pussy.

After a few more minutes, "Okay, one more story," I asked?

"That's all right, we 're both going to flunk out anyway. We should get a ghetto apartment somewhere.

."Stop. Let me tell you something about Trish ....

"Oh, the woman who gives you expensive gifts? Yeah, that's the one I have to hear."

"So ... Trish and Jim are friends of my parents. They had a 30-year friendship that goes all the way back to their years here. When I was a young teen, Trish took an interest in me. She behaved like an aunt or a big sister. No, that's not accurate. It was a Southern California friendship. Trish had become my Obi Wan guide to the adult world. I knew that Mom was watching my actions through Tris.

She's a beautiful Southern California MILF with glittering caramel skin and a voluptuous hour glass body. She's got a pear-shaped butt and long tennis player legs. Big implants and dark eye shadows are the only indicators of her middle age battle. She enjoys every bit of life and wanted me to do the same.

Her husband, Jim, is a great beast of a man. It is an olive-coloured Mediterranean with an unpronounceable last name that started with a P and ended some 15 letters later with a Z or a Y.

It's very flashy: Rolex watches; pink rings and gold necklaces that still seem to be hopelessly entangled in the hair of his face.

Trish warned that I was both pretty and open-minded. They could be easily manipulated. She showed me how to walk in the heels and how to turn my hair back to the flirt. She showed me how to dress 23 when I was 15. She gave me my first pedicure.

She taught me how to know when to stop trouble and when to start it. We went to the Tang Shopping Sprees. I told her about the first boy I kissed, and then the boys I fucked. My first real boyfriend, Tom, had a dick bent to one side and hooked to the other.

"Don't ever give the boy a crooked dick anal," Trish said.

I didn't think so, but it seemed like sound advice. "Thank you, Obi Wan," I chuckled. She did the same thing.

At times our conversations were more intense than that. "Is it wrong for me to masturbate and fantasise about boys and girls? Am I bi?"

"Women are now free to be sexual. We can enjoy the beauty of another woman in the same way as we can appreciate our own beauty while we masturbate. Never deny yourself and never limit your sexuality. I love both the power and the aggressiveness of a man and the sweetness and tenderness of a woman. Sexual pleasure can be accomplished in many different ways."

By the time I reached the age of 19, however, I felt I had learned a lot of things. I was with Tom and his hooked penis, and I was also with Kevin, who had an incredibly thick, thin cock. It felt like I was a can of tuna when I was with him. Trish, however, had prepared a more fulfilling sexual journey. I fell in, but I was more than happy to be my guide on the road.

I worked an odd job a year after high school before deciding that I was ready for college. That spring to celebrate my acceptance at my parents' college, we were all going to Las Vegas for shopping and some fun.

We all came from different parts of the country. Mom and Dad were visiting friends back east and ended up stuck in Chicago because of a snowstorm in the late season. Tom was supposed to join me from Denver, where he was skiing with his buddies, and he was also stuck. Trish and Jim were flying out of San Francisco and doing it all right. I came from Los Angeles and they arrived at the same time. We shared a cab and picked up the adjacent suites at the hotel. I was going to hold my mom and dad 's room so they could be close to their friends, and then I was going to swap out when Tom and my parents arrived.

After check in, Jim hit the tables and Trish hit the store. We had been shopping for a few hours and came back to the hotel with a few bags. We were going to have a shower and get ready for dinner. I found that I was missing a Gucci purse I had purchased earlier in the day.

I knocked at the door of the adjacent suite asking for Trish. She didn't respond, but the door was open so I thought she was in the large suite, so she couldn't hear me. I walked around calling her name. I found that the closet had a few store bags, so I walked over and began to rummage around searching for my purse.

Then I heard about Jim and Trish at the front entrance. Suddenly, I remembered what an awkward situation I was in, so I was hiding in the closet. I might reach the top of the slats in the closet door. I figured I 'd wait for them to leave the bedroom and go back to my suite without realizing it. Jim and Trish had been drinking, and they were about to get there. I was going to have a ring side seat for the best friends of my parents having sex.

I was afraid. And then I got disgusted. And I was so fascinated. And then I was so amused. And then, I was ready. Jim was a Sasquatch: all his hair; his back; his legs; and his arms, which formed into a thick jungle around his crotch. And then I saw his slut. It was so high, damn big. It was darker than the rest of him, as if he had sewed a bull 's dick. I just couldn't believe it was true. Jim lied on his back moaning while Trish licked and slobbered her way up and down in his pipe.

No way, she will handle the beast inside of her. Trish turned around and slowly backed her butt to Jim's chest. She twisted and teased her butt and cunt in the direction of his mouth. Soon he tried to lift his neck to get to her cunt. She scooted a little back every time, so she couldn't get to her cunt.

She turned around and looked at him and grinned and started rubbing her wet pussy against her hairy chest: around and forth from her chest to her stomach, rubbing her pussy against him. After a few moments of poking, the big bear could no longer stand. He moaned loudly, lifted her up by the boobs, and plopped her cunt and back on his chest.

He licked happily at her pussy as she was sucking and grinding him into an even larger erection. They licked and sucked for a few minutes , making the most beautiful sex sounds.

It wasn't like I had the history of moaning and purging and gasping for every caress or licking or sucking. It was so dry, man. I was getting more excited to watch them. I felt better as their lovemaking became more urgent.

I lowered my panties to my knees and began fingering my clit. I was going to cum with them. Trish was ready to move up. Her pussy was softened and lubricated with Jim's saliva, and she slid herself back to the back of the cowgirl. Jim had to let Trish do all his job. She started to lay her back flat on Jim's chest. Slowly, she took the tip of his dick in while massaging her clit.

Jim softly massaged her breasts, kissing her neck. She squatted down and took a little more and then went back to rest her butt on him. She began rocking back and forth on his cock, working longer inside. She squatted herself again and took him all in.

And at the moment when his full dick was swallowed by her cunt, she let go of the pleasure of the pain that gave me goose bumps. Jim realised that he started adding to the enjoyment of taking some of her weight, bouncing her butt up and down on his shaft, I smelled sex in the room; closed my eyes and inhaled, listening to the sounds and pretending that I was part of what was going on.

Then the Godfather 's theme began to play.

Ohh, crap, my cell phone went off. I put down my camera, and the muffled sound came from a place near the bags. I dropped to my knees and searched around in the dark, searching for a blinking light to shut it off, hoping it wouldn't be seen. I found it, and I turned the ringer off.

The door flew open, and all of a sudden I was crouched under a redwood falling into the trees. Jim's dick was long, thick, straight and real.

I burst into tears at the site so close that I ran out of the room with my phone in one hand and my panties in the other.

"What the heck," he bellowed.

"Mike, cover yourself," screamed Trish.

"Jen, Jen, wait for what's going on," she said.

I walked back to my side of the connected suites, slammed and locked, the door fell to the floor and kept crying uncontrollably.

After a few minutes, there was a knock and the voice of a very reassuring Trish called, "Jen, it's me to open the door. It's all right, Jen. I sent Jim down to play Blackjack. Open the door honey."

"I can't ... I can't be so bad for Trish that I didn't mean this the way it looks. I'm so sorry. I'm so humiliated."

"Jen it's all right, really it's all right."

"No," I started crying louder again.

"Jen, I'm going to take a shower. I'm going to try and come back with you in about an hour. Just open the door, then, and talk to me."

Sometime later, there was a knock on the front door.

"Yes," I said to him.

"Room service," was Trish's comment.

"I glanced through the peep hole at her."

She grinned and raised a silver tray with a rose, a bottle of champagne and a bowl full of chocolate-covered strawberries on it.

I smiled, still a little ashamed, and I let her in. She came in and placed the tray over the bed. She was radiant: her hair; her makeup; a little low-cut black dress; and the pumps she picked up earlier that day.

She opened the bottle, poured two glasses of strawberries and said with a really sexy accent." You know, the first time I saw Jim's pecker, I ran out of the room crying, too."

We laughed and drank and ate some strawberries. We ordered a second bottle of champagne. After the second bottle, I didn't feel any pain or shame.

"So what's on the agenda tonight," she said.

"Ah, well, I thought you should spend more time with Jim, after all I did."

"... Don't worry about him ...... the last time I checked his blackjack win ...... he was five grand." Trish called Jim again and asked if he'd join us for a dinner and a show. He was still playing, she said, and he'd talk to us later.

We left the room and were in the lobby before Trish realised that she had forgotten about her cell. I gave her my key card so she could go back to my room to pick it up.

We had a great meal and went to one of the Vegas videos with the girls running around half naked. In reality, Trish knew the producer and we were able to go back to the stage after the show to meet him and some of the girls. We took a break between the shows and stood around in different stages of undressing.

My eyes darted from a direct view to a mirrored image of these beautiful women. I 'd purposely get caught looking at boobs and tits, then face up, and I'd get smiles and winks in exchange. A pair of girls brushed by me in makeup, and I noticed the feathering of our outfit with a faint whiff of perfume.

I was horny when we got back to the hotel. Trish was checking in with Jim. He hasn't left the table yet. We went back to the room for another night cap. I walked in and Trish followed a search to see if there was anything left in the bottles of champagne. She closed one eye and stared at each one of them.

"Nothing left," I said?

"Just a little taste," she seductively put on the top of one of the bottles. Trish has been flirting with me. I felt my ears and my face flush with anticipation.

"You 're not the kind of woman who would be content with a little taste of something," I said.

She smiled and stepped slowly towards me. She stopped right in front of me, staring straight into my eyes. I was waiting to kiss me for her.

Instead, she hit the room phone and asked, "One more bottle?"

"Of course," I said, breathing out very hard. I hope she's realized that.

"So how about sending a few messages?"

"One o'clock in the morning?"

"It's Vegas," she said.

In less than 10 minutes, two more champagne massage tables and two of the cutest Filipino girls arrived to give us massages. The girls had deep auburn shoulder lengths of hair and soft, cute voices. You made them for the sisters.

Trish was in the bathroom, in the bathrobe, on the table, naked in the twinkling of an eye. One of the girls had a towel on her hand. I was following Trish 's lead.

We were lying flat on our stomachs. It was so shockingly dead. The goose bumps grew all over my body, and I was a little ashamed to wonder if my girl had noticed. The girls tenderly caressed us with warm oil while we were drinking champagne.

They massaged my hips, calves, and thighs. I had two choices, either to fall gently to sleep or to orgasm, and to fall gently to sleep. My eyes were closed, and I looked away from Trish.

I've heard a strange rustle, and I'm wondering or, please, this can't be over with you too soon. I opened my eyes and looked in the direction of Trish. She rolled over on her back, and the Filipino girl was massaging her big fake boobies. I must have looked pretty stupid.

"You pay a little extra, and it's a special request, but it's worth it." Trish whispered seductively, closed her eyes and returned to her happiness. The girl massaged her chewing gum drop nipples upright. Her little hands worked the oil around her caressing and gently rubbing Trish's breasts.

Trish has been in love. Oh, what the fuck I was doing. This is how the Roman Empire collapsed, I 'm sure. I took the towel out of my back and looked back at my mother.

"Can you please rub my bum, please?"

My girl nodded and smiled as she remembered my appeal. She had a twinkle in her eye, too, and she held my gaze, indicating that this would be something she had meant for both of us to enjoy. First, she poured the oil over my lower back.

She told me that my ass dimples had the effect of relaxing me. This time she poured again and let the oil trickle down at the very top of the crack of my butt. She picked up the oil and rubbed it in before it burned into my crack. I felt a tingle and I gasped a little; enough for her to hear.

Slowly she poured again. One drip at a time, and let me feel the tingle again. She was caressing me fully. I looked back at her again, arched my back slightly, and the soft encouragement fell upon me with more oil and affection. She was working her way to my inner thighs

My back-end was for both of us to enjoy. Slowly, she examined me carefully to make sure nothing would hurt. She made her way back in and out.

Then she touched my outer pussy lips and rubbed a little bit of dab oil on my clit. She teased my clit around my bung hole for a few minutes, until my butt and pussy begged to be fingered.

At the same time, she entered both of my openings. Slowly she slipped in and out of me agonizingly slowly. Each stroke is a little deeper. Then rotating each hole, and then working together. I shuttered and walked out loud.

Trish reached out and stuck out my hand as I was cumming. After a few minutes, she said, "Happy endings are another add on the hun."

"Yeah, god it's a little worth it I thought. I truly believed the girls were happy working on us. They gave us a lot more than half an hour. They gave us a business card. Trish paid the messages to the room but gave each girl at least two hundred and fifty bucks in cash as well.

I say, it was soo worth it.

We were alone in our robes again. "Well, thank you for that night. It's the best date I've ever had." I crawled over to her. She sat down and looked at me a bit. I reached up and placed my hand behind her head and pushed her lips against mine.

We hugged each other for a few seconds. She pulled my dress around my shoulders and started nibbling at my neck and licking my face. She whispered to me, "Are you ready for the next step in your journey, baby?"

"Yes." She stood there and let her dress drop to the floor. I kissed her stomach and I worked my way down to her clit. I kissed her a bit. She put her arms on my back and told me to stand up. I stood there, and I dropped my robe on the floor. We've been wearing a tight hug for a few seconds. She took my hand softly, and we walked over to the bed.

I was a little anxious and overwhelmed by Trish's prowess, but she put me at ease. She was so caring and gentle, and it was really my first love to witness. She was sweet and caring, and she asked me how I felt about it, or if I liked it.

We were chatting and we made love. Without me doing much of anything, she coordinated our orgasms so that we both fell asleep exhausted in each other's arms.

The first rays of the sun were running over my forehead.

I was lying in bed. "Trish, wake up. What's with Jim? I 'm sure the poker game is over. He 's got to be looking for you right now"

She put her hand around my head and gently pulled me down to her and then kissed me. "Baby doesn't worry about him, I 'm sure he had a very entertaining evening," she whispered.

"What is it?"

"Jen, he's been in the closet watching us all this time."

"Nooooo, my GAWD."

"Would you like him to join us," she said with a little laugh?

"Trish, no, not his giant ass. It's too much. I'm so tired now, and I'm so afraid of it."

She chuckled again and pulled back her hair. "Well, maybe next time you have some rest. Why don't you give him a full eye for me before you leave? Get up and go to the bathroom. I'm going to pretend to smuggle him out."

I rolled off my bed and turned and crawled back to give Trish a nice kiss last night. I arched my back so that my butt was up in the air in front of the wardrobe. Jim had a good view of me from behind, and he could see what it was like to have me doggie.

I kissed Trish a few more times, not wanting to leave the moment. I stopped, thinking about Jim staring at me in the closet. I was dreaming about his beautiful cock and my butt covered in baby oil begging him to come in. I was wondering what he was thinking.

"And that was my first Trish and Jim story."

Paige had been playing with herself all the time, and had surrendered in the open mouth when I ended my story.

"That's it," asked Paige, more than a little disturbed?

"That's exactly what we have to get to college."

"Bitch," he said.

Self-righteous Slut

It had been a while but, as expected, Lara called me with an excuse of having to talk to me. Her arguments, still being upset after our seemingly one-night stand and other such frivolities, she really just wanted to make me understand, but without ever being direct, that she wanted to have sex with me again and would be happy to fulfill my every wish or fantasy.

"You know where I live, you come by Saturday afternoon at three, and I recommend you don't dress like a secretary or a slut," I told her dryly and firmly as if to remind her who was leading the show.

I remedied the wait by remembering our only encounter, and how easily she submitted to my every wish, including that of playing with her in the lobby of the building where she lived. I also remembered the beauty of her ass, and the pleasure I had felt sodomizing her several times, without too much excess or violence. As I began to feel that I could also smell her sweet perfume, but just as the nostrils were searching for that taste in the air, the doorbell rang.

She showed up, in perfect time, with a black and white sheer dress that ended right under the knee. It made her look quite sexy, at least at first sight. For me, who knew well the curves that hid under that dress, was the portrait of desire and sin. We sat down on the sofa, and immediately she started talking about what she didn't like about our first meeting, about the fact that it wasn't so easy for her, tied together with meaningless sentences.

"Why don't you stop shooting shit, undress me and allow me to enjoy you," I told her, cutting off her umpteenth pointless statement.

"You're not listening to me," she timidly protested as I took off my jacket.

I slipped a hand through her hair, then pulled her face against mine, and kissed her with such vigor that it took her breath away. My lips slipped slowly over her neck, and my hands along her thighs, coming to brush against her panties.

"From this point on you will obey me because that is what you want," I whispered in her ear as I nibbled at her earlobe. "From you, I just want to hear yes and never no, otherwise look for someone else look for someone else, but I promise you they will only think of their own pleasure and never yours."

Lara said nothing, but her lips searched and found mine, and what followed was one of the longest kisses I can remember. I let her take off my blouse and bra, allowed her to kiss my nipples until I decided to take up the reins of again. I pushed her back making her lie on the sofa and then put myself on top of her and covered her not only with my body but with kisses and caresses, especially on the mouth and neck. When I slipped the dress off of her and left her only with a bra and a little chaste thong, my field of action became every inch of her skin above the navel. Her moans increased in intensity as soon as I moved her panties a little, to stick her finger in the now soaked palace of her desires.

"You're just a slut ready to give it to everyone to enjoy," I said almost tearing off that beautiful thong that had only become a hindrance. "But now I want to drink your pleasure directly from the source, and see how long you resist before you squirt in my mouth."

I pulled up my skirt just enough to be able to kneel between her thighs, wide open. I was finally able to lick that nectar that flowed copiously from her. She was biting her lips more to distract herself and not cum in a short time than to stifle screams from the pleasure she was feeling. Her resistance to orgasm, however, collapsed as soon as I put in not one, but three fingers into her vagina, bring her immediately to capitulation.

"Now that you've finished being the naughty slut, allow me to enjoy some," I said sitting on the sofa. "That is, as long as you don't want to go out as you are and show everyone your beautiful ass."

Even if mine wasn't a real threat, Lara did not lose a moment to kneel next to me and undress me leaving me with the only my knee-high stockings on, kissing every strip of skin she discovered as she was taking off my clothes. Her mouth then rested on mine to descend slowly into my thighs, where I stopped her by pressing her head against the lake of my desire.

But I could not say anything, because she slipped three fingers into my pussy almost angrily, in a way that I enjoyed. However, it was at that same time that she was seemingly deciding to give in to her future fate as a submissive. In fact, I brought myself to orgasm without obstructing her in any way, enjoying at the same time the thought of her next humiliation.

"Brava, my slut, who always knows how to make me enjoy," I said leaving her appalled after having enjoyed the peak of pleasure. "Now put your dress back on, because we are going to go out to do some shopping, but forget your panties, you won't need them."

" But this way I'll leave myself exposed," she protested in an unconvincing manner.

"All the more reason to keep your legs closed, as long as you can."

To make sure she obeyed me, I went to dress, taking her thong with me, to come back to her who was clearly embarrassed.

"Can I ask where we are going," she asked me as I closed the front door.

"To buy a nice rubber dildo so I can screw you as much as I want," I replied making her believe I was joking.

I actually took her to a porn show where I put her in embarrassment, not just talking about the importance of measuring a good dildo, but by repeatedly touching her all over her body. At the end of our outing, I bought a big strap-on, a couple of smaller dildos and a nice plug with a colored crystal in the middle of the handle. I did not have time to close the door of the house, after a trip in the car done in silence, that Lara almost threw herself at me, trying to assert herself.

"You can't treat me like that!" She screamed angrily "I'm not your whore and I don't do everything you want. From now on I...."

I didn't let her finish the sentence as I kissed her, then pushing her against the table.

"You are my bitch and you will do what I want," I told her raising her dress and thus baring her butt. "And what I want is to put on that strap-on and smash your ass in two. It is completely useless for you to try to affirm the contrary because it is what you want too, then stop breaking the rules and do what I say."

We found ourselves clinging in a long kiss, and while our tongues intertwined in endless games, my hands exposed her breast.

"You know that when you come to me you will do what I want most," I whispered in her ear before going down with my mouth to one of her nipples. "But tell me who you were with after our meeting."

"With no one! Because I did nothing but think of you and find the courage to call you."

"Do you know why you did not get fucked by anyone," I asked, passing to the other nipple with little bites but without hurting her, "because with me you are what you are, a slutty lesbian who likes to obey and take it in the ass."

I made her lie down on the table to roll her dress up around her waist and take off her bra, I then resumed kissing her in the mouth, but only after putting my hand between her thighs.

Lara was now in my possession, but I didn't want to just subdue her, I wanted to make her enjoy it. So, I slowly descended from her mouth until the beginning of the split, but once I arrived, I decided that she still had to wait to enjoy.

"Come down from the table and lick me good, I want to be warm before I screw you," I told her, slipping off my dress and then leaning against the table.

She obeyed with some disappointment, but then it was clear that I was the one leading the game. Lara moved my panties and finally discovered my lake of pleasure where she covered it with kisses before running her tongue through every groove of it, making me pant with pleasure.

"Mm, how good my bitch is," I murmured moaning "Give me more pleasure otherwise I won't give I will only pleasure you from the ass because I know that you can't wait for me to put you on all fours and take that sweet tight ass of yours."

I made myself go to the threshold of orgasm, before ordering her to take the strap-on I had just bought. First, she stared at me and then without saying anything she simulated a full-blown blowjob.

"See you know you belong to me," I said pushing all of the phallus between her lips. "As soon as you see a big one, you take it immediately in your mouth and it doesn't matter if it's real or made of rubber. But now you just have to play games, lean against the table and open your legs well because I really want to have fun."

The girl obeyed almost enthusiastically, but as soon as she was in position, instead of screwing her I started kissing her enthusiastically at the crux of her body that place of pleasure, while at the same time slipping my fingers between the labia majora. Lara bent her legs to almost fall when I penetrated her with two fingers. But I didn't give her the time to get excited because I replaced my fingers with the strap-on phallus, which slipped into her wetness smoothly. Again, I didn't allow her to utter a single moan as I changed, sodomizing her completely with a couple of decisive lunges.

"I enjoy it!!! Fuck how I enjoy! He shouted as he grabbed the table as if he were afraid of running away.

"Of course, you enjoy," I replied, penetrating her pussy again "And don't worry I want to fuck you till I am exhausted."

I kept changing the opening to fill with my strap-on, making her have a couple of orgasms and then went to sit down in my comfortable black armchair in order to give myself some rest. But Lara was of a different opinion and stood over my weary body to sodomize herself.

"Let me enjoy it again," she said, taking my hand to bring it to her dripping flower of pleasure.

I answered her request by slipping two fingers into her and using what little energy I had left to thrust into her deeply, although it was she who dictated the rhythm, more than I could. I decided to let her have some control over the situation before resuming command. I was waiting for her third orgasm. Once that was achieved, I made her lie down on the carpet to resume my mode of operation of switching insertion between both her naughty little holes.

"Let's see how much you can take from me," I told her after yet another sodomization.

When I gave it to her, I moved calmly, sometimes kissing her in the mouth and feeling her breast. When instead I slipped the phallus into her rectum, I was more impetuous, so much so that sometimes the strap-on came out of the little hole, giving me the opportunity either to change the entrance or to sodomize it completely with new vigor.

"Paige, please, my ass is on fire," she said, looking for mercy.

"Shut up and take it or I'll have a new punishment for you."

Actually, she was both tired and eager to have my orgasm too, so soon after I stood up, took off my strap-on to go sit down back in the armchair.

"Now come here and make me enjoy it," I told her, pointing to the center of my legs.

She approached walking on all fours and then resumed licking my center of enjoyment with more enthusiasm than before as if she couldn't wait for me to cum so that she could go home. Despite all her mastery, I did not give in quickly, wanting to enjoy every pass of her tongue or touch with her fingers inside my lake of desire. To delay the orgasm as much as possible, I began to insult her and suggest that she meet a friend of mine. That my friend would screw us together as a couple and that the meeting would make her release her inner whore. I thought about how Amber could have abused her, making her even more submissive than she already was. I could easily see the image in my mind of Amber and I doing such perverse things to Lara, using her like a sex doll. In the end, I succumbed to the supreme pleasure, wrapping me in my orgasm, while Lara's tongue slowed her passage between my intimate lips.

"Put on your dress and go away, but leave the rest here," I said almost pushing her away with one foot.

"But with nothing underneath," she asked me in surprise as she stood up.

"Do you still not understand who you are, slut? But if you want, I will give you back your panties, but only if you go out with a nice plug in the ass, and believe me I will choose a nice big one, just to keep the hole wide open."

After being sodomized for a long time, Lara the option of the plug was off-putting. So with a little disappointment, she put on the dress without panties.

But inside of me, I knew that the idea of a three-way relationship was already whipping around her head and that I would see her again very soon.

Lydia with Jack

Lydia rolled her eyes, muffled laughter cumulating under her breath as she looked towards Jack, knowing what was to come. "Open Sesame! Or is it Says-a-me?" questioned Jack, waving his hands wildly at the threshold of his apartment door.

"How many more lives do you think that joke has left before it fizzles out and dies?" questioned Lydia sarcastically. A smirk formed on her face as she reached out and unlocked the door to their apartment. She and Jack had been dating for nearly a year, and somehow, she had managed to laugh her way through the majority of it.

"Two or three, give or take," quipped Jack, reaching out and putting his hand on Lydia's shoulder. "Four or five if I space them out just right." Lydia shook her head, her smile never fading as Jack led her into the living room. Despite her rolling eyes and muffled laughter, she enjoyed every moment of Jack's quirky humor.

"This is what I get for dating a magician," she laughed. Jack looked back at her, giving her a subtle wink as he removed his jacket. Lydia followed suit, undoing the belt of her cinched, red trench coat and hanging it up on the hook that sat on the wall near the door.

"I never get tired of seeing you in that thing," said Jack, turning to look at Lydia. She was adorned in a tight-fitting leotard, rhinestoned to the nines. It sat cinched at her waist, showing off her figure, and flattering every curve. The low-cut front positioned itself in such a manner that her cleavage was always somewhat on display while providing ample support for her full breasts.

"This old thing?" questioned Lydia sarcastically. Jack chuckled, nodding his head as he reached out and popped the strap atop her shoulder. Lydia had been working as Jack's assistant for some time, and over the last year, their relationship had developed from friendship, and co-worker, to that of lovers. Despite several shows a week, Jack wasn't lying when he said he never grew tired of seeing Lydia wearing her uniform. The tight leotard clung to her body just right. Although he didn't want to admit it, there had been many times during one of their shows that he found himself struggling against the erection trying to form in his pants.

"You know there's only one thing I like seeing on you more than that leotard, right?" questioned Jack, bringing his other hand up to rest on Lydia's shoulders. "My favorite thing to see you wear is nothing at all." Lydia giggled, no stranger to Jack's brand of humorous flirtation.

"Well, you won't be seeing that standing here," she returned, reaching up and grabbing at his hand. With a smile, she turned back to Jack, as if to suggest he follow her. Jack nodded his head, knowing what was to come. With a grin prominent on both of their faces, the two lovers made their way towards the bedroom. By the time they made it to the door, Jack was already feeling a throbbing in his groin. He gave Lydia's shoulders a light squeeze, almost pushing her forward in an attempt to get her into the bedroom even faster. Lydia didn't delay, she was just as eager as Jack, even if she didn't show it on her face.

After a few moments, they entered the bedroom, wasting no time shutting the door behind them. Although the bedroom itself was quite simple, artifacts of their show were littered about, giving the bedroom a unique scenery. Lydia made her way towards the bed, hopping off the floor with her heels, and landing on the mattress. Jack watched her with a smile of adoration. It was not only her sexy body, and witty humor that made him fall in love with her, but her mannerism, and way of doing things as well.

"What are we in the mood for tonight?" questioned Jack, his eyes wandering over Lydia's body as she made herself comfortable on the bed.

Mmm, Lydia moaned, taking a moment to think. "I'm thinking Act II, illusion three."

"You read my mind," said Jack reaching up to quickly undo the buttons of his shirt. One by one his fingers gripped the buttons and pulled them apart. There was no denying he was eager, based off the speed of his movements. With a happy sigh, he tossed his shirt aside, watching it land haphazardly atop an elongated black box, one of the many tricks they had been working on together in their spare time. With a similar pep in his step, he moved forward, crawling onto the bed.

"Let's get you prepared," Jack continued, reaching down and grabbing once more at the straps of Lydia's leotard. Lydia maneuvered herself against his grip, helping him to slide the straps downwards. Jack could feel his fingers fidgeting with anticipation as he carefully peeled Lydia's leotard away from her body. Inch by inch the fabric descended, exposing more of her skin by the minute. As the costume reached her ankles, Jack gathered it in his hands and tossed it across the room, watching it land atop his shirt. Leaning forward, Jack firmly planted his lips against Lydia's. If there was anything he loved more than seeing her dressed in her costume, it was seeing her take it off.

Lydia returned his kiss with delight. As his lips pressed against her own, she felt her breathing start to hasten. She parted her lips slightly, allowing space for her tongue to emerge and push carefully into Jack's mouth. She could feel Jack's fingers grasping tight to her shoulders as her tongue met his. Back and forth their tongues glided as their lips met. A subtle moan escaped Lydia's mouth as she leaned back into the headboard, feeling her heart starting to beat faster in her chest.

Jack wasted no time working to remove the rest of Lydia's clothes. He reached behind her back, skillfully unclasping her bra with one hand, and pulling it forward with the other. It slid off her chest with ease, releasing her breasts from their containment. Jack grinned, leaning down and lightly nipping at her exposed nipples. Lydia gasped, looking down at him, her breath becoming harder, and faster. "Lean back for me," whispered Jack, leaning forward to speak quietly into her ear. Lydia nodded her head, doing as she was told.

Before she had time to react, she heard the clicking of a collar around her neck. Her gaze cast upwards as she looked at Jack. He seemed all too thrilled to see her there, her movements restricted by the leash that lead from the collar to a bolt above the headboard. Lydia reached forward, grabbing at Jack, but it was to no avail. The moment her hand grasped firmly to his chest, a popping sound radiated around the room. Jack chuckled, moving back out of Lydia's grasps, watching as her arm fell to the bed, completely removed both from his chest, and her shoulder.

Jack's smile grew even wider as he reached down, lifting the disembodied arm from the bed and holding it in his hand. From where he stood Lydia could no longer reach him as the locked collar around her neck severely limited her reach. As Jack held tight to her arm, it hung limp in his hands. He carefully trickled his fingers up and down the length of it, fondling it lightly as Lydia watched. All she could do was sit there helplessly as Jack fondled the limp arm from top to bottom. "I like you better all pulled apart," he said.

Keeping out of her reach, Jack extended the arm forward. He used it to stroke Lydia, the limp fingers gliding over her legs. "Let's make sure you can't keep putting up a fight, then we can get to the real fun," suggested jack. With another chuckle, he tossed the arm to the end of the bed before approaching Lydia once more. Lifting his hand into the air he twisted his fingers to the right and then to the left. As he did so, the lighting in the room began to dim, casting shadows of various shapes and sizes along the walls. With another flick of his fingers, the radio began to play in the background, filling the gaps of silence in the room with smooth music.

"Now the other hand my dear," said Jack with a smile as he reached forward swiftly, grasping tightly to Lydia's other hand. In the dimly lit room, a haze of green light could be seen emanating from his fingertips as he pulled at Lydia's other arm, removing it as well from her body. Now, with both arms removed, and a leashed collar holding her firmly in place, her ability to resist him was severely limited. "Open your legs," he commanded, casting his hand upwards. With his words, Lydia felt two leather belts from beneath the bed swing upwards and wrap around her ankles, pulling them apart with ease. Her eyes opened wide in surprise as she looked at Jack, the smile on her face still as prominent as ever.

With her disembodied arm still in his grasps, Jack leaned forward, using the limp, lifeless fingers to glide along Lydia's skin, moving from her hips to her toes. The fingers glided with ease, limply caressing her skin as he guided the movement of the arm. Up and down one leg, then up and down the other. After a moment Jack lifted the arm, using the backside of the hand to carefully stroke Lydia's cheek. Watching her sitting there helpless riled him up like nothing else, and for Lydia, there was nothing else quite as exhilarating.

After a moment of caressing her soft, delicate skin, he cast the arm forward, pushing it between her legs. Lydia watched carefully as her own fingers made contact with her groin through her panties. She could do nothing but watch as Jack manipulated them, gliding them up and down between her legs. Her entire body quivered. There was nothing quite like the sensation of your own hand teasing and pleasing you, while you have no control of it. Jack exhaled sharply, moving closer to her now. She was in no positioned to fight back, so he made himself comfortable, sitting between her legs. "The more you lose, the more fun this becomes," he said with a smile, meeting Lydia's eyes.

Reaching down, he grasped at Lydia's panties. He held them firmly, pulling forward with a strong grip. Lydia gasped as she felt the back of her underwear be pulled deeply into her backside, gathering like a thong at the back of her ass. "Oh!" she gasped feeling the tension against her skin. With wide eyes, she tried to adjust her sitting but before she knew it a loud pop echoed around the room as her panties were torn from her body. Jack chuckled, holding them tightly in his hands. "Hold these for me," he suggested, leaning forward and stuffing them into her mouth.

With her panties removed, and firmly situated in her mouth, Jack could get a better view of the space between Lydia's legs. Despite her gasps and groans, it was no secret she was enjoying herself. Jack could see the wetness already starting to form at the forefront of her vagina. Her labia was swollen with excitement and anticipation, perhaps in part from the stimulation of her own severed fingers. Reaching forward again Jack guided the limp fingers of Lydia's disembodied arm towards her groin. Lydia moaned quietly through the cloth of her panties as she felt her limp, lifeless fingers slide up through her slit. Her body shook as her groin pulsed, her labia and clitoris swelling to their full potential.

The fingers slid up and over her clitoris, then back down again, lifelessly dragging over her skin. Although there was no rigidity to the fingers, their friction alone back and forth over her clitoris still filled her with pleasure. Jack kept going for a few moments before setting the arm aside. He was ready to jump into the action himself, doing more than just teasing Lydia. With swift hands he quickly began to undress, tossing his remaining clothes to the side. Much like Lydia, he himself was a very attractive man. Despite his quirky attitude and odd sense of humor, Lydia was immensely attracted to him, especially when he was fully in control. "I want to have a little fun too," Jack said, reaching out and gently rubbing Lydia's restrained leg with the tips of his fingers.

Now undressed, Lydia could see just how much fun he was having. It was no surprise to her that he was already hard and throbbing with anticipation. All she could do was sit there and watch as Jack took up her arm once more shifted its position on the bed. He moved it closer to him, palm facing up, before laying his cock in Lydia's hand. Although she could feel nothing, something about watching her hand being used, with no ability to stop it, turned her on even more. Jack was enjoying himself as well as he took the lifeless fingers and curled them around his cock, holding his hand over the top of them to keep them curled. He gave Lydia a devilish grin as he pumped his erection in and out of her severed hand, as she sat there watching.

With his other hand, he gestured upwards, reaching towards the chain that held to Lydia's collar. Slowly, as he began to raise his hand, the chain pulled upwards, raising Lydia off the bed by her neck. She gasped through the panties in her mouth her cheeks quickly turning red. Jack groaned, continuing to rub his cock with her disembodied palm as he watched her lips begin to turn purple. With no arms to catch herself, and her legs firmly belted on either side of the bed she was left to hang there struggling to breathe. With each second that passed her body trembled more and more until with a quick gesture of his hand, jack sent her back down to the bed. Mmmph, was all Lydia could muster as she fell back hard against the mattress.

As Lydia worked to regain her composure, Jack took up her arm and tossed it to the side. "Let's move on if you don't mind," he said smiling with glee as he reached for her legs. Lydia closed her eyes, knowing what was coming. There was a familiar popping sound as both legs were swiftly pulled, releasing from her body. Jack grinned in absolute delight as he held up the legs, one in each hand. Looking at Lydia now, all he could focus on was how helpless she looked, sitting there with no limbs at all. It filled him with such excitement, he could barely contain himself. "I have a better idea."

Adjusting his stance, Jack crawled back up onto the bed. Lydia wasn't sure what to expect as he approached her, reaching into her mouth and removing the panties. For a moment she opened her mouth as if to speak, but Jack was having none of it. Having been already well prepared, Jack swiftly opened the bedside table, and from within it pulled out a metal and leather O-ring gag. Lydia cocked her head to the side, a subtle smirk appearing on her face. Jack leaned in, quickly pushing the metal of the O-ring into her mouth, before fastening the leather strap behind her head. With the device in her mouth, she was completely unable to bite down at all. Her mouth was forced open, held in a circular position.

Jack quickly stabilized himself, carefully standing up on the bed between her legs. Lydia watched as his cock approached her face, but there was nothing she could do. Jack reached down and grabbed at her hair, pulling it slightly as he rubbed his cock along either side of his face. He took in the sensation of his shaft grinding along one side of her cheek and then the other as she sat there unable to move. Taking a deep breath, he repositioned himself in front of her, before slowly inserting the tip of his cock into her forced open mouth. Lydia exhaled slowly, able to taste his pre-cum already on her tongue. She could feel him firmly holding her head in place as he slowly slid his erection into her mouth. She could feel him slowly grinding against her tongue and the roof of her mouth as she took in the taste of him.

As Jack began to pump in and out of her mouth, he reached down and toyed with her nipples. He rotated his fingers around them, pleasing and teasing them, enjoying the feeling of them growing hard against his fingertips. Inside of Lydia's mouth was warm and moist. With each pump he pushed his cock further down her throat, making it hard for her to breath. His hands continued to pull, twist, and squeeze at Lydia's nipples, making her entire body tremble. With no arms and no legs to fight back all she could do was sit there and take every last bit of it.

In and out, in and out Jack continued to thrust, enjoying the feeling of Lydia's mouth to its fullest. After a few minutes, however, he withdrew himself, wanting to ensure that he lasted long enough to fully pleasure them both. With a smile, he slowly got back down to his knees, before laying down between Lydia's legs. He could feel her entire body trembling as he extended his tongue forward and placed the tip of it against Lydia's swollen clitoris. She gasped, already moaning as he started to lick her. His tongue journeyed up and down her slit, paying special attention to her clitoris. He flicked, licked, and rotated his tongue, causing Lydia to moan like mad through the O-ring gag. Her body jerked and twitched, overwhelmed with pleasure as he licked her over and over and over again, but after just a moment, he quickly pulled away. "I was just trying to get you wetter my dear," he suggested.

Lydia raised her brow, unsure what he meant until an overwhelming sensation took hold of her. She gasped in pain and pleasure as she looked down to see Jack, inserting the rounded end of her arm into her vagina. If she had toes to curl, she certainly would have as she felt her own arm enter her. The end of her arm was bigger than Jack's cock but not too terribly much. It was just enough to cause her pain and pleasure all at once. Jack looked down, enjoying watching as he began to thrust her arm in and out of her, moving slowly, careful not to hurt her. Lydia moaned and groaned as the saliva that accumulated around her gag dripped down onto her arm, lubricating it further.

Jack continued to thrust the arm in and out of her slowly for several minutes before carefully removing it. The grin on his face was still prominent as he tossed the arm aside, back into the pile with the other arm, and her legs. There was no hiding the utter delight on his face as he reached up and grabbed Lydia by the hair, holding tight and pulling it firmly. She moaned and groaned through her gag as jack bent in, opening his mouth and bit down firmly on her neck. Lydia's eyes opened once again as she felt the pleasure and pain flow through her. As he pulled back, Jack could see the circular indenture of his teeth still left in her skin. His cock throbbed hard with excitement as he groaned, pulling upwards, his hands glowing.

Another pop was heard as Jack released his grasp, watching as Lydia's head fell to the bed. He could hear her gasping, and trying to speak through her gag, but he knew she only wanted more. Although her head was severed, her eyes still followed him as he picked up her head and forced it down on his cock. Reaching outwards he laid his hand upon her body, sparking it with his magic. As he forced her head up and down on his cock, her body continued to breathe, and pump blood all on its own. His magic coursed through it, leaving it operational, and capable of feeling all sensation.

After his cock was nice and wet again, he repositioned himself on the bed. He sat Lydia's head on top of her stomach, forcing her to watch as he laid her body down carefully and got on top of it. Lydia watched on with fear and excitement as Jack thrust forward, his cock entering her pussy right in front of her eyes. She could feel everything as he entered her, wasting no time thrusting deep and hard. With one hand he kept his balance on the bed, and with the other, he held tight to her head to make sure it wouldn't fall. Back and forth, back and forth he thrust his hips, pushing into her hard and fast. Her heart beat faster in her chest, and her breath hastened as pleasure filled her body to the brim.

Jack throbbed inside of her, her tight, wet pussy pleasuring him fully. He pumped in and out of her for several long minutes before moving up to his knees and thrusting into her upright. As Lydia watched on, enamored by the pleasure she suddenly felt Jack pull her head up once again. "Lick it," Jack commanded as he turned her head around, thrusting it forward into her own pussy. With a few flicks of his fingers, he quickly undid the leather strap around her head and tossed the gag aside. Lydia groaned, moving her mouth around, stretching it in every direction. Jack held tight to her head pushing her forward once more. "Lick it, Lydia," he said once more.

Lydia gasped lightly, extending her tongue. As Jack thrusted the full length of his erection in and out of her, she was forced to go down on herself. She focused her tongue on her clitoris, rotating it in circles, and licking back and forth. She timed each lick with a stroke of Jack's cock, keeping rhythm perfectly. Although her body could not move, it could feel every bit of sensation as it was used. Lydia closed her eyes and focused on her own pleasure as she licked her pussy. Jack groaned and held tight to Lydia's head as he thrusted in and out of her in long hard strokes. He could feel the walls of Lydia's vagina growing tighter, and tighter on him as she was pleasured by both his cock and her tongue.

The bed bounced against the wall as he thrusted harder, faster, and stronger. He felt his cock throb deep inside of her, filling her with even more pleasure. The head of his erection slammed against her cervix with great force, making her entire body rock up and down on him with ease. All the while Lydia continued to lick at her clitoris, so filled with pleasure that she could barely think of anything else. Able to still feel all the sensation in her body, she was overwhelmed with how good everything felt. Her mind was almost numb with pleasure as she continued to lick at herself furiously occasionally extending her tongue downwards to rub against Jack's shaft as he pumped himself in and out of her.

The more she licked the closer she felt herself growing to orgasm. The heat and intensity were building up inside of her more and more every second that passed. Her nipples were standing on end, her clitoris was swollen, and she was being licked, and fucked like she couldn't believe. Shockwaves of pleasure and delight were forced through her entire body as her disembodied head continued to aid in her own pleasure. Jack moaned and groaned as well slamming his cock deep inside of her and reveling in the feeling of her tongue occasionally grinding along his shaft. He could feel himself throbbing with pleasure as he was drawing nearer to orgasm as well.

After a few more minutes he pulled out of her, keeping her head cast downward to force her to continue licking. She was so wet that he slipped right out with ease. Without warning he bent forward, readjusting his angle and pushing the head of his cock against her ass. Her eyes opened wide with surprise but before she could react, she felt the full length of him slowly slide into her. She gasped several times, trying to get back into the proper rhythm as Jack pushed into her. Jack reveled in delight at how tight she was as he pushed the full length of his shaft into her.

Now with more space for her head, Jack lowered her down slightly. As she continued to lick at her clitoris, she also took the time to extend her tongue and force it into her own pussy. With each passing second, she was getting closer to orgasm and she was sure Jack was too. She could feel Jack picking up speed, his cock throbbing deep inside of her, signaling that he was going to cum soon. Back and forth, in and out he pumped, taking long strokes and focusing on his pleasure. Lydia focused on her own as well as her tongue licked wildly against her pussy.

It was almost a race to the finish to see who would cum first as both of them were so incredibly filled with pleasure that they could focus on nothing else. Jack's moans and groans mixed with Lydia's filling the dimly lit room. Both of them were going crazy, drowning out the sound of the soft music playing in full. Lydia could feel her pussy throbbing, causing contractions to start in her abdomen. Her pussy and her ass tightened as she felt herself about to lose control. Jack could tell she was about to orgasm as she tightened around his cock. He did his best to keep pumping in and out as the added pressure simply pleased him more.

Suddenly, Lydia could take no more as her entire body fell hot. The contractions lasted longer and were closer together as she started to cum. Her pussy pulsed with pleasure as she came, doing her best to moan and breath all while licking herself, riding out the orgasm the best she could. She was overwhelmed with pleasure, panting and struggling to keep control as the shockwaves overtook her, sending one stroke of excitement over her body right after another. For several long seconds, she licked and licked until she finally exploded, reaching a peak of pleasure of which she could take no more. She gasped for air, her tongue finally falling limp inside of her mouth as she tried to catch her breath.

Jack was only pumping in and out of her harder now. The feeling of her tightening, contracting and cumming all over his hard cock only brought him quicker to orgasm as well. He felt his cock throb with delight as he pushed himself in and out of her ass. Lifting her head up into the air, he held her by the hair, letting her head dangle so she could watch him continue to thrust into her. Lydia watched on, moaning quitter now as she watched Jack keep thrusting in and out of her. She could feel his grasp tighten as he started to reach the point of no return.

With several more, hard thrusts forward Jack felt himself reaching completion. His shaft throbbed from based to head as he suddenly felt the rush of pleasure he too had been awaiting. With great force, he came, shooting wet, warm semen forward and deep into Lydia's ass. She moaned once more, able to feel the sensation of the warm liquid enter her fully and deeply. Jack pushed forward, staying as deep in her ass as physically possible until he felt every last drop of semen leave his body and enter hers. All she could do was continue to lay there helplessly as he finished inside of her, reveling in the pleasure.

After a moment of trying to catch his breath, Jack was finally able to pull out of Lydia. She groaned as she felt the fullness leave her body. She could finally breathe easy again as she looked up at him, her disembodied head smiling softly, though obviously tired. Jack sighed looking down at her, a genuine and happy smile growing on his face as well. With his hand he reached out and gently stroked Lydia's severed head, massaging her scalp lightly with his fingertips. Trying to catch his own breath he slowly sat back down on the bed, her pile of discarded limbs on one side of him, and her core on the other side.

"That was nice," he said softly, picking up Lydia's head and setting it down on his lap. With gentle strokes he ran his fingers through her hair, trying to give her time to settle down before moving her around too much and making her any dizzier than she already was. For several long minutes, they sat there together with Jack stroking Lydia's hair. Lydia stayed quiet, her eyes closed as she focused on Jack's hand gliding through her hair and massaging her softly. "Did you have fun?" he asked, looking down at her with, lifting her hair up and out of her face. He could tell she was giggling quietly as he swooped her hair out of her eyes and over the back of her head. "I'll take that as a yes," he said, nodding and standing her head still in his hands as he turned to look back at the bed and all of the discarded parts haphazardly strewn about. "Well my love, I guess it's time to put you back together."

One Friday Night

Jim and Karen lived a few doors away from their best friends Peter and Wendy. All were in their mid-thirties and had known each other since college and had spent many holidays and social events together since then.

One Friday night, they found themselves in a group of eight at a wine tasting with several neighbors from the immediate area.

The wine had loosened a few tongues, and some of the questions became quite personal.

"You four are out with other people, that makes a change," came a comment referring to Jim, Karen, Peter and Wendy.

"We mix in larger groups, go out as a couple, as individuals, but as a group of four we have many common interests," Karen explained.

"Is one of those common interests a bit of bartering?" asked Matt, who talked about a bottle of wine over his limit and a big mouth at the best of times.

The group groaned in embarrassment, although secretly many would have liked to know the truth.

"There was nothing to report, no exchange of any kind," Peter offered.

All this had put a damper on the party and our four left early and went to Jim and Karen.

Jim put a bottle of wine and four glasses on the coffee table.

"We've all had enough wine, but just in case..."

They were all quiet for a while because the wine tasting had been disappointing.

"We gave them more ammunition when we left, now they imagine us all naked and lying in a heap on the carpet," Wendy remarked.

"You cannot control what other people imagine," said Peter.

"I can't blame them, I know what I would think if I were outside the group," Jim said.

"Are we all as pure as the driven snow, does anyone here want to confess that they have thoughts about another person in the group?

They were quiet for a while, then Karen spoke up.

"Remember that holiday in Scotland, it was Edinburgh, an Indian and a Chinese restaurant had been recommended, but we couldn't agree on where to eat. I took Peter and Jim to Chinese, and Wendy went to Indian.

"I reached for the soy sauce and rubbed my arm against Peter's arm, I held his arm and slowly pulled him away. That set me on fire, I think if we hadn't agreed to regroup later, I might have apologised by taking off my panties.

That was a wild thing to do by group standards. Not to be outdone was Wendy had a story to tell.

"We were on this cruise in the Mediterranean, and I hurt my foot. It was splinted in hospital, which made walking in the old cities quite a challenge. The three of them kept holding a hand or an elbow to give me support. I loved holding hands with Jim, I wore the splint and bandages longer than necessary.

Peter was next: "My weakness is to mentally undress Karen. In the unlikely event that I ever see her breasts or pussy, I wonder if they will look the way I imagine them to.

"That's no secret," Wendy said, "I often wonder if your intense looks will set her clothes on fire.

"That just leaves me," said Jim, "I keep dreaming of being shipwrecked with Wendy on a small tropical island. We never get over the problem of sand in our genitals."

"We are not quite as tense as we thought," commented Wendy.

The girls seem to like holding hands, it sounds very innocent, will someone change places?" Peter asked.

Peter and Karen made themselves comfortable on one two-seater, Jim and Wendy on the other.

They came closer and felt the warmth of their partner's thighs, held hands and talked quietly.

Peter and Karen's lips came closer and closer as they whispered. Jim and Wendy did the same. Each couple watched the other's progress. When the kissing began, there were no objections.

Karen climbed onto Peter's lap. Wendy immediately followed with Jim.

Karen opened her blouse: "You wanted to see if my breasts were the same as they appear in my dreams?

Peter reached for her and let go of her bra.

"In my dreams they were perfect, and they're even better in real life."

Jim was now kneeling on the floor in front of Wendy on the sofa with one hand on each thigh under her skirt, sucking on her nipples.

No one else dared to go on that evening, they ended the evening as if nothing extraordinary had happened, and Peter and Wendy set off for home.

They did not meet again until Sunday afternoon, when they went for a walk in the country and ended up at Peter and Wendy's house.

It was obvious that they needed a debriefing and a plan for the future, but they were all unusually reserved.

Jim broke the ice: "That was a great evening, my heart rate still hasn't normalized. Can I assume that we will all stay with our current loving spouses, with the possibility of further 'exchange' initiatives?

"Well said," Peter said.

The ladies both nodded in agreement and looked very pleased with themselves.

Peter and Jim decided to watch the rest of a game on TV, the ladies went into the kitchen to heat up some snacks and put on the coffee.

The game was over, the smell of coffee and food poured in from the kitchen.

Peter and Jim sat relaxed in their chairs, completely unprepared for their next surprise.

The ladies each came in with a tray of food and coffee - they only wore bras and panties.

"Remind me to tip the waitresses, Peter, lovely young girls," Jim asked.

"Peter has seen me naked on his bucket list, he's seen my breasts tonight, he might see my pussy. Karen explained.

"I suppose Jim and I will keep up with you - or go ahead," laughed Wendy.

Jim and Peter carried the trays back into the kitchen and put the dishes in the dishwasher.

When they returned to the family room they were presented with a wonderful sight. The ladies were naked and practicing dance steps to background music.

They asked the boys to sit down.

"Undress before you make yourself comfortable," Wendy demanded.

"Sorry, we're hopeless at dancing to stripper music and totally incompetent at lap dancing, but we'll do what we can," Karen explained.

"That's great, don't apologize," said Peter on behalf of the male audience.

Karen stood up on Peter's chair, lap dancing style, with one foot on each side of his thighs. That brought her pussy up to his face level.

"As beautiful as in your dreams?" she asked.

"Perfect." was all Peter could say.

"I wanted to split the lips of my pussy to show all my wealth, but I have to keep my balance, would you assist me, please?

Peter gently parted her pussy lips with his thumb and forefinger.

"I only have a tiny clitoris, maybe you can make it grow with your tongue," she invited.

Peter reached both hands, spread her pussy lips and tried to bury his face.

Jim and Wendy were at the same stage on the adjacent sofa.

The ladies changed their position and sat down on the boys' laps to kiss and touch each other.

"We can't leave you with angry erections," Wendy said, "I'll look for tissues and oils or lotions and hope that handwork is enough for the grand finale tonight.

Wendy instructed Jim to lie on his back on the floor and she overcame him in the style of 69, giving him a short lollipop before applying oil generously. He stuck one finger of one hand into her pussy and grabbed a breast with the other hand.

Karen had Peter on her hands and knees. She stood under him and turned down to suck his cock. Then she moved and positioned her breasts under his cock. Partly hand-fucked and partly tit-fucked, he made a deposit between her tits. Karen rubbed him against her skin and licked her fingers clean.

Jim and Karen went home, past the four neighbours who were also at the last party. They were standing in front of one of their houses, each with a glass of wine in his hand.

There were exchanged pleasantries, Jim and Karen felt suspicious.

"If they only knew what we've been up to lately," Karen laughed.

Within the group of four, nothing was said or discussed about the following weekend, except that they were to have lunch at a fish restaurant, followed by coffee and cake at Jim and Karen's place.

Maybe coffee and cake is a euphemism for coffee, cake, oral and vaginal sex?

In the middle of the afternoon Jim and Peter were in Jim's workshop when the ladies called them into the house. Wendy took Jim's hand; Karen took Peter and they went upstairs to the second and third bedrooms.

Wendy and Jim undressed quickly, he put his arms around her, grabbed her bottom and was up and in her before she reached the mattress. It lasted less than a minute.

"She laughed, "You have to catch the bus?

"Without that I would have been bursting at the seams, now I'll do anything you want, at your service.

"I'll finish off with a back and front massage with two fingers in the pussy and French kissing, then I'll ride you cowgirl. After that we will cuddle and sleep until we are hungry enough to go downstairs at six or seven.

Peter and Karen had a different approach. They kissed and cuddled on the bed before they undressed.

"Karen asked: 'Kiss and lick me from top to toe with special attention to my tits and pussy. If you do a good job, I'll do something similar to you. Then we'll decide whether we'll fuck first and then take a nap or take the nap first and then fuck before we go down for dinner.

That night, everyone agreed that they were anxious to fuck their spouses when they returned to their own beds, but they admitted they would fall asleep before anything happened.